F
Hay

Hayes, Daniel
No effect. Godine [c1993]
288p

Tyler finds adolescence even more difficult when he falls in love with his teacher, who is dating the wrestling coach, and in an effort to win her love, he tries out for the wrestling team

1 School stories 2 Wrestling--Fiction
3 Teachers--Fiction I T

ISBN 0-87923-989-1
LCCN 93-29329
008825 58-106-02 860632 ME © BAKER & TAYLOR Books 4092

NO EFFECT

Also by Daniel Hayes

The Trouble with Lemons

Eye of the Beholder

✦ NO EFFECT ✦

– by –

Daniel Hayes

David R. Godine · Publisher
Boston

First published in 1994 by
DAVID R. GODINE, PUBLISHER, INC.
Horticultural Hall
300 Massachusetts Avenue
Boston, Massachusetts 02115

Library of Congress Cataloging-in-Publication Data
Hayes, Daniel.
No effect / Daniel Hayes. --1st ed.
p. cm.
Summary: An eighth grader joins the wrestling team
and has his first crush on a teacher.
[1. Schools--Fiction. 2. Wrestling--Fiction. 3. Teachers--Fiction.] I. Title.
PZ7.H3145NO 1993 93-29329 [Fic]--dc20 CIP AC
ISBN 0-87923-989-1

FIRST EDITION
Printed and bound in the United States of America

NO EFFECT

✧ I ✧

THERE WERE A ton of reasons why I shouldn't have gone out for wrestling. Even *before* I found out the Coach was some kind of lunatic. For starters, I'm not all that tough. I'm a good runner and I've always kept myself in decent shape, but those things didn't seem to help much when it came to fighting. In the past year alone I'd taken a few pretty good beatings from kids, and the thought crossed my mind that wrestling could end up being nothing but a way for me to have regular beatings built into my schedule. And I wasn't thrilled about the idea of putting on that goofy-looking protective headgear they make you wear—probably because some wrestler once had his ears ripped off or something. Plus I'd always heard that wrestling coaches make you lose about fifty pounds right off the bat. Which meant I'd be wrestling toddlers.

But none of these thoughts really sunk in. I still went out for wrestling.

I hadn't given it that much thought beforehand. After all, eighth graders don't usually get to go out for any high school sports. So it came as kind of a surprise in music class that afternoon when Mr. Blumberg got on the P.A. and announced that they needed more kids for the wrestling team, especially lightweight kids, and that anybody who wanted to, even eighth graders, could try out. All you had to do was get a permission slip and a physical.

Mr. Blumberg no sooner got done announcing this than a folded up piece of paper came flying across the aisle and skipped off my desk and onto the floor. It was from Lymie. Music, which we only have twice a week, and art, which we have the other three days, are the only classes besides gym that Lymie and I are together in. In most of my classes I'm accelerated. In music and art it doesn't matter—we're all pretty much remedials there.

I checked for Mr. Fritz before I reached down to grab the note. He was resetting the needle on Haydn's *Surprise* Symphony. He looked kind of annoyed because he'd just given us this whole spiel about how Haydn had stuck a surprise in the symphony to keep everybody in the audience awake, and Peter Kawecki had asked him if Mr. Blumberg's announcement was the surprise. Mr. Fritz didn't even answer. He just frowned and concentrated on resetting the needle without scratching the record.

After the music started up again, I worked the note in closer with my foot until I could grab it, and then I opened it behind my pile of books. It said, "Hey, Ty, you going out for that?"

I had to smile. I mean, who else but Lymie would start a note with "Hey"? When I looked up, I noticed Mr. Fritz was smiling at me and nodding his head. It took me a few seconds to realize that the violins had all of a sudden gotten louder, which was the surprise, and Mr. Fritz must've thought that my smile meant that I got a kick out of it.

As soon as Mr. Fritz closed his eyes and seemed to go back into his own little world, I looked over at Lymie's chubby, expectant face and shrugged. Lymie grabbed another scrap of paper and started in on it. The way he was hunched over the desk with his face all scrunched up, you'd think he was writing a novel or something. He folded the note, did a quick Fritz check, and flicked it at me. This time it said, "You're scrawny enough."

I looked back over at him. He was all cracked up.

"Moron," I whispered across the aisle. "Butthead..." Then my mouth froze in its tracks. Mr. Fritz had picked the needle off the record, and I was waiting for him to start yelling at me for talking.

"Wasn't that a surprise, boys and girls?" Mr. Fritz said in his still-in-his-own-little-world voice. "Imagine someone about ready to drift off right there in his seat and—bang—that crescendo of violins. Let's play that again." He bent down to reset the needle.

Lymie grabbed some more paper, scribbled down something, and flicked it at me. This one said, "Were you just talking to yourself?"

I looked at him. He was all cracked up again and pretending to thump on his desk. I smiled and leaned back in my seat. I had some serious thinking to do.

There's two sides to any argument. I went over the plus side of wrestling first.

To start with, I could get a letter. And getting a letter in eighth grade—that'd be nothing to sneeze at.

Second, it'd probably make me stronger. I'd always wanted to be better in the strength department, and wrestling would give me a pretty good workout every day.

And there was a third reason. It was nothing more than a daydream really, but I'm pretty sure it was the thing that sold me on the whole idea. All the rest of the afternoon, whenever I'd think about being on the wrestling team, I'd get this picture in my head, like a recurring vision or something. I'd see myself lying on the mat, pretty much unconscious, but not completely. I'd be delirious and everything, but some part of me would still be able to see what's going on. And what's going on is that all the girls in the stands are going crazy because they're afraid I'm not going to be all right. And while the coach is lifting my head trying to get me to come to, and while the team doctor's trying to get a pulse on me, I can see all my teammates looking worried and beating their fists into their hands and swearing what they'll do to the other team if one hair on my head has been harmed. After a while, the coach and the team doctor hoist me up and start to lead me off the mat. The crowd is going crazy cheering. The girls in the stands are jumping around, and I notice most of them have tears in their eyes. Before I leave the mat, the referee comes over and lifts my arm in the air, and I hear the announcer telling everybody that I'm the winner because the kid I was wrestling had done something illegal, which was the only reason I got hurt in the first place. Then I'm helped into the locker room for medical attention. And even after the door closes behind us, I can still hear the cheering.

Of course, even while I was having this vision, some other part of me started shouting "Baloney!" and telling me all the reasons why I shouldn't go out for wrestling. First of all, I might *really* get hurt. Sincerely. Broken bones were a real possibility...and hernias...and brain damage...the list went on and on. And team doctor? Like they were going to hire a doctor to go to every wrestling match and wait for somebody to get hurt.

That only pays for the big spectator sports like football, or maybe basketball. Which leads us to the cheering crowds. Any dimwit knows that unless you're in the Olympics or something, wrestling crowds consist of a few parents and a couple of kids who probably missed their bus. And girls? What kind of girls go to wrestling matches anyway? Girls who like violence? Or maybe emotionally disturbed ones who get their jollies seeing you get stuck in some kind of crazy python hold that'd probably prevent you from ever having kids unless you adopted some. Which led my mind to remind me of my main fear: humiliation. Every sport—every activity even—has its humiliation potential, but wrestling's got to be the big daddy of them all. There you are, out there all by yourself in tights (they're kind of like tights anyway) with some guy you don't even know trying to twist you into funny pretzel shapes for the amusement of some crowd. Only it's not a crowd. Luckily.

My mind struggled with all this for the rest of the afternoon. Once I almost decided to chuck the whole idea. Then all of a sudden there it was again—my vision. Bigger and better than ever. I'm being led off the mat. Women are going crazy. Not even girls now. Real women. And not disturbed ones either. Nice, normal women who are all beautiful. And they've all got tears running down their faces. And every tear has my name on it.

I grabbed a permission slip off the office counter before I went home.

"Case closed, Tyler. The answer is no."

I followed her into the kitchen. I didn't have any real game plan. It was only a week ago that I'd gotten in pretty bad trouble over something Lymie and I did that was *supposed* to be just a little joke but kind of backfired, so I knew I wasn't in any great bargaining position. I figured my best bet would be to try to wear her down with whining.

"Why not, Mom? You can't just say no like that without even discussing it."

Mom planted her feet and looked me in the eye. "I think we've had enough trouble with you and fighting. And as far as I'm concerned, wrestling is another of those sports that sanctions and glorifies combat. Not only am I opposed to the idea philosophically, but I think it's dangerous. I'm not going to let you do something where I'll have to worry every minute that you'll get hurt."

"Mom," I said, "listen to reason, will ya?" I cut around in front of her as she headed for the cupboard. "Did you ever hear about something terrible happening to a wrestler—like he got hurt really bad or dropped dead on the mat or something? You always hear about things like that in football. And boxing—sure. And even in basketball sometimes somebody'll drop dead in the middle of a game. But wrestling, Mom? Be real." I stuck my face in front of hers. "Come on. Look me in the eye and tell me you've ever heard of anything like that happening to some wrestler."

"No," she said, staring me right in the eye. "And that's no on the permission slip too." She yanked her face free and brushed past me.

"Maybe you're thinking of professional wrestling, Mom. You know—Lex Luger, Damian Demento—guys getting hit with tennis rackets and stuff."

"No, I'm not," she said as she rummaged through the cupboard. "Case closed."

"I think we need a little objectivity here," I said and grabbed the phone. "Chris'll talk some sense into you."

I heard Mom give this big sigh as I dialed my brother's number. I got his answering machine and remembered it was still the middle of the day in Los Angeles. So I dialed Chuckie's number. Chuckie's our groundskeeper, and you can tell just by how he's built that he's into sports. I'd seen him going into his cottage on the far side of our property when I got home. Almost before he got to say hello, I started in on him, telling him about Mr. Blumberg's announcement and how wrestling could help build up my strength and earn me a letter and everything. When I was done, he said, "Sounds great, Ace."

"Yeah, it would be," I told him, "only I can't get Mom to sign the stupid permission slip. You gotta talk to her, Chuckie. Tell her how good it'll be for me."

"No can do, Ace. I just work here. I'm not gonna start telling your mother how to run her house."

"How to run her house!" I squeaked. "Chuckie, what are we talking about here—choosing curtain colors? This is my life!"

"Sorry, pal. But you'll have to work this one out on your own."

"Chuckie, it'll take like two seconds. Just tell her she's being foolish and to sign the thing. I'll put her on." I started to wave Mom over.

"I gotta go, Ace. My phone's ringing."

I heard a click. Right after a chuckle, which was because he knew I knew he didn't even have call waiting. I looked at Mom. Her arms were folded and she was kind of hunkered down, ready for anything.

"Yeah, that's what I tried to tell her," I said into the phone. "It's the safest thing in the world... Huh? Oh, yeah, I know how women get... Yeah, you're probably right. She'll probably come around on her own... Okay, yeah. Thanks, Chuckie."

I hung up the phone. Mom came sashaying over to me, clamped her thumb and forefinger around both sides of my jaw, and squeezed. "No," she said right in my face. "No, no, no."

I looked at her. And it finally dawned on me. She'd really made up her mind. I'd lost. It didn't matter what I did. I could kiss my letter good-bye. I could kiss my recurring vision good-bye. Suddenly I felt sad.

"Fine, Mom." I pulled my jaw free and started to leave. "Forget it." And then in the doorway I turned to her. "You know, Mom, it's not fair. Seriously."

She had her arms folded again. And she was hunkered down again.

"Other kids probably have mothers who won't sign their permission slips either," I said. "But they just go to their fathers to get 'em signed. But I don't have a father." I looked her right in the eye. "And that's not fair."

I had to get out of there quick. I thought I might start crying.

Before dinner I heard this little knock at my door, and Mom came in holding the permission slip.

"I signed it," she said and handed it to me.

I sat up on my bed. I felt strange. Bad strange. It's funny—I try all kinds of things to get what I want, and sometimes they work and sometimes they don't. But what I'd said downstairs was the God's honest truth. And yet now I felt guilty. Like I'd cheated or something.

"I'm sorry I said that," I told her.

"I never would have signed it," she said, pointing at the permission slip. "Partly because I don't like fighting, but mostly because I'm scared to death you might get hurt. But your father loved sports...and you're right, he would have signed it." She walked over to the door and stopped. "And he would have done his best to be there for you at every match."

I sat there holding the thing in my hand until Mrs. Saunders called me down to dinner.

The physical was the last step. And the coldest. It must have been fifty degrees in the nurse's office. Of course, it's hard to feel all cozy and nice when you're standing around on cold linoleum in nothing but your underwear. It was make-up day for winter sports physicals, so there were only five of us lined up in front of the doctor. The nurse was behind us at her desk facing the other way. I wondered if she was checking us out whenever nobody was looking. I know if there were girls behind *me* getting physicals, I'd be sneaking peeks like crazy.

But freezing in my underwear around some nurse who might be a Peeping Tom was the least of my worries. All the other kids were clutching their permission slips. I had a permission slip plus a stack of medical records I could've knocked out a moose with. Mom's idea. Or more like Mom's orders. She thought the doctor should know about my allergies...and my asthma...and my history of migraines... and how I'd dislocated my shoulder when I was eight. I even had a record of all my shots—maybe in case I bit somebody or something. I was afraid the doctor would take one look at my medical history and tell me to hit the road.

Somebody bumped me from behind. Then I heard this voice say, "Hey, John Henry, you gonna wrestle or play basketball?"

It was the big guy in back of me—Ox Bentley, our star linebacker during the football season. I didn't know him personally or anything, but everybody knew who he was.

Next something thumped me between the shoulder blades.

"Hey, John Henry, you deaf or something?"

It was Ox again. And he'd been talking to me. I looked at

him. "I'm not John Henry," I said. I tried to say it nice. When football players, especially seniors, start talking to junior high kids, it usually spells trouble.

"Isn't that your name?" He pointed to my waistband. "John Henry," he read slowly.

I looked at him again. I couldn't tell if he was putting me on or not.

"No," I said. "That's just the manufacturer."

That cracked him up. "You're all right," he said, clapping me on the shoulder. "You're all right, John Henry."

Just then the doctor finished with the kid ahead of me—a kid Ox probably called Hanes. I stepped forward and handed him my papers. He tossed them on the table behind him, cranked my head around, and shined a light in my ears, first one side and then the other. Next he listened to my heart for a minute. Then he did it. I knew he was going to, but I still wasn't ready for it. He pulled my waistband out, reached in, and came up under my left gonad. I took a hitching breath as he applied a little pressure.

"Cough," he said, and pushed my head sideways with his free hand.

I did it.

"Again," he said, coming up under the other one.

I did it again.

He pulled his hand out and rapped me on the arm.

"Next," he said.

And that was it. I swear to God, you could have cancer, rabies, bubonic plague, and two broken legs, and you'd pass a school physical if your ears were clean, your heart was beating, and you had a couple of cojones that felt halfway decent.

So I was in business. I was now officially ready to wrestle. And

I felt pretty good about it. It wasn't only the women in the stands part. I knew that was just my imagination working overtime. And it was more than getting a letter, or building up my strength, or anything like that. It was...I don't know...a feeling like I was a part of something bigger than myself. And that no matter how tough it was I still knew that I was a part of a bunch of guys working together for one common goal: victory. Like guys going off to war, only we wouldn't have to kill anybody, just pin them. It was a good feeling, a feeling of belonging, with maybe a dash of prestige mixed in. I noticed as I was walking out of the school with Lymie that I was even walking a little straighter, a little taller. I was part of a team—a real high school team.

"So you're really gonna do it?" Lymie said. "You're really gonna wrestle?"

I looked at him. And I tried not to seem too proud, too smug. "Yeah," I said. "I'm gonna do it."

Lymie looked back at me. "Whaddaya wanna spend your free time rolling around the floor with a bunch of guys for?" He shrugged and started for his bus.

I stood there. I didn't grab him or argue with him. I didn't even call him anything. I just stood there and felt all that sense of belonging to something bigger than myself—with maybe a dash of prestige mixed in—schlump back to wherever it hides most of the time.

"Later, Ty," Lymie called back over his shoulder.

"Yeah," I told him, "later."

✧ II ✧

"EVERYBODY HERE TODAY HAS MADE A DECISION. AND IT MAY BE THE MOST IMPORTANT DECISION OF YOUR LIFE."

The Coach and his big potbelly strode back and forth in front of the bleachers. About fifteen of us sat there gawking at him. I was glad I was in the back. His voice could just about knock you out of your seat. This was our first meeting—or rather my first meeting. The real first meeting was Monday, but the Coach stormed out when he discovered he didn't even have enough kids to fill up all the weight classes. Now it was Wednesday and there were three new kids: me, Ox, and this freshman named Justin who had a Southern accent.

A few minutes earlier the Coach had taken Justin and me into the locker room to weigh us. Ox didn't need to come. He'd wrestled before. Plus everybody knew Ox'd be a heavyweight.

"Let's see what we got here," the Coach said and yanked Justin toward the scale. "Ever wrestle before?"

"Not on a team, sir," Justin rolled off like a soldier—a Confederate one.

The Coach stepped back and kind of curled up his nose a little and shook his head. I couldn't tell if he thought Justin was being wise with the "sir" or if he just didn't like the twang.

"Get up there," he said and jabbed his thumb at the scale.

Justin stepped up on the scale platform. The Coach started sliding weights around.

"One-ten," he said. Then he started feeling Justin's arms and pinching his stomach and stuff like he was a slave trader or something. "We'll take you down to ninety-eight."

I looked at Justin. He already looked pretty skinny to me.

"You—get up there," the Coach said to me. I got up on the scale. It didn't budge. The Coach slid the little weight down to zero. Still nothing.

"Are you on there?" he barked.

I looked at where my feet were. "Yeah," I said.

He slid the big hundred pound weight to zero and pushed the little pound weight up the other way.

"Judas Priest," he said. "Eighty-nine, for Chrissakes. And that's with clothes on, and shoes on, and probably money in his pockets." He looked at me. "You got money in your pockets?"

"A little," I said and showed him a five-dollar bill. Like a jerk.

He kind of winced. Then he shook his head. "You know, all the other guys at ninety-one'll have dropped a lot of weight to get there, and you...well, we'll have to build you up and see what happens." He felt my shoulders and rapped on my stomach a few times. "They'll rip you to shreds," he said and then thought for a minute. "All right, listen up. In addition to working harder than you've ever worked before, I want you to eat a big, fat, juicy steak every day, ya hear me? Every day."

"I'm a vegetarian," I said.

He sucked in some air and kind of bent his whole face up. And as he walked out I could hear this groan come out of him, kind of weak and pathetic, like the sound somebody makes coming to after being knocked out.

I think he groaned again when he looked up and saw all the kids sitting in the bleachers, although I didn't hear anything. But all during his speech he was still wearing that expression he had when he left the locker room.

"BY SHOWING UP HERE TODAY YOU'VE DECIDED TO PUT YOUR LIVES UNDER MY CONTROL." He jabbed both thumbs toward his chest. "MINE!" He dropped his hands to his hips and checked us out in the bleachers. He stood there for a minute, giving his disgust time to sink in. "AND IT LOOKS LIKE WE GOT OUR WORK CUT OUT FOR US. JUST LOOK AT YOU. A BUNCH OF GIRLS!" He kind of spit out the word "girls" as if it tasted bad.

A few of us sneaked little glances at each other to see if we were as pathetic as he said. I couldn't tell. I was starting to get that nervous feeling in my stomach I always get when I find myself in a situation I dread. You know, my first day at a new school, checking into a hospital, waiting to get beat up...that kind of thing. And the weird thing was I was doing *this* voluntarily.

"JUST LOOK AT YOU," the Coach continued. "WRESTLING IS FOR MEN, AND I DON'T SEE NOTHING HERE BUT GIRLS."

He glared at us again. We all looked at our feet. I tried to talk my stomach into settling down.

"DO YOU KNOW WHAT IT MEANS TO WRESTLE?" the Coach was yelling. "CAN ONE OF YOU GIRLS TELL ME THAT?"

He waited. I held my breath and hoped he didn't call on me.

"THE NAME OF THE GAME IS PAIN, GIRLS! THAT'S WHAT WRESTLING MEANS—PAIN!"

My stomach scrunched up inside me. I knew the dictionary wouldn't back him up on his definition of wrestling, but my stomach wasn't thrilled at the prospect of spending an entire season with a coach who thought like that. Plus I was starting to feel pretty alone. Isolated. I didn't know one other kid on the team. Not really. All of them were high school kids and most had been on the team before. But the worst thing, the scariest thing, was that most of them, at least from the looks on their faces, seemed to think the Coach was normal. I wanted to quit. I hadn't even been to a real practice yet and already I wanted to quit. At least part of me did. The other part of me wanted to kick my own butt for being such a wuss. The part of me that wanted to quit was thinking about throwing up. I looked down as the Coach's bald head strutted by.

"PEOPLE DON'T LIKE PAIN ANYMORE!" the Coach was yelling. "THEY'RE AFRAID OF A LITTLE PAIN!" He made a U-turn and strutted back the other way. "PANSIES! THAT'S WHAT WE'RE RAISING, A GENERATION OF PANSIES!" He stopped in front of the center of the bleachers and glared up at us. "THAT'S WHY I STILL DON'T HAVE ANYBODY TO WRESTLE AT ONE-O-FIVE. CAN YOU BELIEVE IT? NOT ONE LOUSY KID IN THE WHOLE DAMN SCHOOL TO WRESTLE AT ONE-O-FIVE." He paused, shook his head, and looked up my way. "AND LOOK WHAT WE ENDED UP WITH AT NINETY-ONE! WE RAIDED THE NURSERY FOR CHRISSAKES!"

I felt about five million eyes turn my way. I gulped.

"AND WITH MY LUCK HE'LL BE RIPPED TO SHREDS AT OUR FIRST MEET AND I'LL HAVE TO

FORFEIT FOR THE REST OF THE SEASON!"

I gulped again. It's a miracle I didn't puke. Even the part of me that had wanted to kick my butt for being a wuss wanted to pack up and leave now. Only I couldn't move. I just sat there hoping I'd evaporate.

"BEFORE YOU GIRLS LEAVE HERE TODAY," the Coach continued, "I WANT THE NAME OF A KID—ANY KID—WHO CAN WRESTLE AT ONE-O-FIVE. YA HEAR ME? I WILL NOT FORFEIT THAT WEIGHT CLASS ALL SEASON. I DON'T CARE IF HE'S OUTTA SHAPE. I'LL GET HIM IN SHAPE. I DON'T CARE IF HE'S OVERWEIGHT. I'LL CUT HIM DOWN TO SIZE. JUST GIVE ME A BODY. GIVE ME A BODY AND I'LL DO THE REST." He was quiet for a minute. "I'M WAITING, GIRLS!"

A few kids came up with a couple of names, but it turned out the kids they were talking about were all way too big. The Coach took down their names anyway, probably in case one of our regulars got hospitalized or something during our first practice.

"I'M STILL WAITING! DON'T ANY OF YOU GIRLS KNOW ANYBODY THAT WEIGHS UNDER ONE-TWENTY? IS THE WORLD GETTING THAT FAT?"

Nobody said anything. I sat frozen, staring at my feet, but I could hear the Coach's footsteps down in front.

"McALLISTER!" That was my name. I looked up. "WHAT ABOUT IT, McALLISTER? WHAT ABOUT THAT EIGHTH-GRADE NURSERY? THERE MUST BE SOMEBODY DOWN THERE THAT WEIGHS UNDER ONE-TWENTY. I'LL EVEN TAKE ONE-TWENTY-FIVE. I'LL WORK HIM DOWN TO ONE-O-FIVE. DON'T YOU WORRY ABOUT THAT."

I still can't believe what I did. There I was, trying to concentrate on not puking all over the bleachers, and praying that this guy would just let us go, or that the police would come for him or something, so that I could get out of there and never have to see him again—when all of a sudden—I still can't believe it...I gave him Lymie's name.

✧ III ✧

LYMIE STAYED OVER that Friday. The Coach had already talked to him about joining the team. I don't know what the Coach said, but it worked. Lymie signed up. We figured we'd get a head start on getting ready for our first practice on Monday by getting in a good workout on Saturday morning.

I thought Lymie would be pretty mad at me, giving his name to some wrestling coach, since he'd already made it clear what he thought about wrestling. And since Lymie and I belt each other all the time over diddly day-to-day stuff, I thought something like this might result in me taking a serious pounding. But when Lymie came running up to me on Thursday telling me how the Coach had talked him into joining the team, he seemed happier than I'd ever seen him. At first I was afraid he might be faking it, and when I let down my guard he'd cram his fist down my throat. But it never happened. He'd gone to the doctor's office for his physical on Friday, and he was all psyched to start getting into shape.

Of course, I'd have to break it to him before Monday how

the Coach might possibly be an escaped psychopath or something. Plus set him straight on a few other things. Like how the Coach was a big fan of pain. And how he liked calling us girls. And how he expected Lymie to lose twenty pounds.

The weight thing alone might blow the whole deal. See, in some ways Lymie's kind of like a lower animal. I don't mean that in any nasty way or to be disrespectful to him or anything. He *is* my best friend. It's just that Lymie doesn't think ahead that much. You know, plan for the future like some people do. He's more into instant gratification. Take his average day: A big chunk of his free time is spent looking for food. Then there's the time it takes him to eat it. And then there's his TV time. And the time he spends looking around for girls. Or at girls anyway. Neither of us had made any real moves yet. But the point is, I really didn't think Lymie could sacrifice eating or sitting around in front of the TV or leering at girls, or that he'd be willing to beat his body into shape, all for some goal way off in the future. I wasn't even sure I'd be able to do it.

I climbed into bed before ten because I wanted to get up early and get started on our workout. Lymie was sitting on the foot of my bed. That was the way it usually went when Lymie stayed over: He'd sit there talking to me until I fell asleep, and then if he couldn't wake me up, or if I started getting too mad about being woke up, he'd go over to my brother Chris's room to sleep. Chris is only around for holidays and stuff, so his room is usually empty. Late at night was when Lymie was most talkative. And tonight was no exception.

"Hey, Ty?"

I had just closed my eyes. "Yeah?"

"What'd ya think of that doctor?"

"I don't know," I said. "He seemed like a pretty regular doctor." I knew what he was getting at. I knew Lymie pretty well.

"Nothing strange about him?" Lymie said. "He didn't do anything strange?"

"Nope," I told him. It was quiet for a minute, but I could feel Lymie's eyes on me.

"Didee grab 'em?" he said finally.

"Did he grab what?" I knew what, but I always do that to Lymie. I don't know why. To bug him, I guess.

"You know," he said and pointed at himself, "the family jewels. Didee grab 'em?"

"Whaddaya think? Yeah, he grabbed 'em." I propped myself up on my elbows. "I got a physical, didn't I? Same as you."

Lymie studied my face. "Why?" he asked. "Why'd he do it?"

"It's part of the physical," I told him. "They always do that."

"Man," Lymie said. "When his hand came up under me like that, I figured he must be some kind of weirdo. My regular doctor just looks. You cough and he just looks."

"Yeah, well your regular doctor might be the weirdo because any doctor I've ever been to feels 'em."

"What for?" Lymie said. "What's that got to do with wrestling?"

"They're looking for hernias and stuff. You know, like ruptures from lifting heavy things. My brother told me. And if you've got a hernia or something and you're wrestling, the first time you pick some kid up, well..." I kind of waved my hand.

"Well what?" Lymie wanted to know.

"I don't know," I said. "You can really hurt yourself, I guess."

I lay down again. Lymie was quiet for a while, so I closed my eyes and rolled over.

"My mother goes to a lady doctor," Lymie said.

"Big deal," I said into my pillow. "A lotta doctors are ladies now."

"No, Tyler. I mean a *lady* doctor. A guy doctor who only sees ladies."

I rolled back over and looked at Lymie. "That's crazy," I said. "Why would he only see ladies? Isn't that discrimination or something?"

"I don't know. But that's the way it is. I swear to God."

I sat up. This was strange. Usually I was the one who knew stuff.

"So if a guy makes an appointment, they won't take him?" I said.

"No, 'cause he doesn't do guy medicine. My mother told me. She said women go to him for female reasons."

"Yeah?" I said. "Female reasons?"

"Yeah," Lymie said. "Whatever that means."

I thought about it for a while.

"Wait a minute," I said. "Yeah, I get it now."

"What?" Lymie wanted to know.

"Think about it, Lyme. We have things that girls don't have, right? And girls have things that we don't have. Get it?" It felt good to be in the driver's seat again.

"Get what?" Lymie said.

"Look," I told him. "If a doctor who was trained to work on guys tried to feel a girl like he did us, he'd be kinda outta luck, wouldn't he?"

Lymie's face lit up. "I don't know about that," he said and started cracking up.

"Cut it out, Lymie. I'm talking about a doctor, not some butthead like you. Think about it. What do girls have that doctors would need to check?"

Lymie sat there for a second trying to think. Then it dawned on him. He got all happy looking and cupped his hands in front of his chest.

"Yeah," I said. "Breasts! Didn't you ever hear of a breast exam?"

"Wow," Lymie said all wide-eyed. "Some doctors get to do that all day!"

I let out a sigh. I could feel another one of Lymie's big career moves coming on.

"Don't go getting all excited, Lyme. You have to put in eight years of college, and you have to study like twenty hours every day. Whaddaya think, they just let you walk in and start examining women?" I lay back down, figuring the idea of that much studying would put an end to our conversation.

"Wow," was the last thing I heard Lymie say before I drifted off. I didn't know if he was thinking about all the studying or if his mind was still back on breast exams.

The first thing we did on Saturday was to run. We went to the track at school, which I usually don't do. I'd rather run through town or out into the country where you can get the feeling of covering some distance and take in some scenery besides. But Lymie was no runner, and I figured by being at the track we could stay kind of together without me having to cut my usual pace.

Lymie surprised me right off the bat by doing two pretty decent laps. I mean, he wasn't breaking any records or anything, but he was chugging right along for a kid who was kind of fat. I lapped him after my fourth and noticed he was breathing pretty hard, so I slowed down until he pulled up next to me.

"You oughta walk one, Lyme," I told him. "It's not good to overdo it your first day."

He shook his head. I think he even tried to crank on some more speed.

"I'm telling you, Lymie. You gotta be sensible. I've been

doing this for a while. To start in you should walk one lap for every two you run. Any fitness coach'll tell you that."

The fitness coach thing did it. Lymie slowed to a walk. "I'll just catch my wind," he said. "You don't need to wait."

I took off. I was starting to feel pretty good. Four laps had just warmed me up. This was my first November in upstate New York and after living my whole life in L.A. I wasn't all that crazy about the cold weather, but today the cool damp air felt good on my lungs. I felt like I could run for hours. I did another twelve laps—three miles—before I decided to call it quits. We had other training to do.

Lymie wouldn't leave till he'd finished two miles, so I chugged around with him and then we rode our bikes back to my house so we could start in on our strength training. I figured it was a good time to start breaking the news to Lymie about the Coach. It wouldn't be fair to let him show up for practice on Monday expecting to be coached by somebody human.

"So, Lymie," I said as soon as we got up to my room, "what do you know about Coach Robilatto?"

"Whaddaya mean?"

"Like when he came to see you, did you notice anything strange about him?"

"Like what?"

I sat on the side of my bed. "Like was he chewing on somebody's arm or something?" I looked at him. "Lymie, I gotta tell you. This guy is like no other guy you've ever seen in your whole life. He yells all the time. He calls us girls. He likes pain..." I was counting all his major personality traits on my fingers.

Lymie laughed. "Tyler, he's a *coach*. What'd ya expect—Mary Poppins or something?"

"No," I said, "but I didn't expect Genghis Khan either."

Suddenly Lymie's face got all serious. "You're not thinking of wussing out, are ya?"

I shook my head. "I'm definitely gonna do it," I told him. "I just thought *you* should know what *you're* getting into."

"Yeah, right," Lymie said and punched me in the arm. "If anybody wusses out, it'll be you."

"We'll see who wusses out, dirtbag," I said and punched him back.

Lymie wanted to start right in wrestling and build our strength that way but I said no. I knew how that'd go. Lymie'd slam me on my back about eighty times and knock the wind out of me, and then while I was busy turning purple, he'd pin me. He'd get in shape, and I'd get in pain. And knowing the Coach, I figured I'd get to experience pain soon enough.

We ended up doing the usual stuff: a few rounds of sit-ups, push-ups, and some chin-ups on a chin-up bar I'd put in the doorway of my room. I couldn't believe how hard Lymie worked. He went all out. I'd never seen him like that. No matter how much of anything I did, he did more. I always knew Lymie was stronger than me, but I'd never actually seen him go to the limit like this before. He'd do sit-ups until his face was all red, and then he'd go right on to something else. The only break he took was when he had to wait for me on the chin-up bar, and then he bobbed around on the balls of his feet and shadowboxed. Only by some strange coincidence, the shadow he was boxing was always a quarter inch in front of my face. All while I was going up and down on the bar, I could feel the breeze from his fists. I ignored him, figuring that'd be the best way to handle the situation. Besides, Mom always tells me I should work on maturity, and ignoring Lymie seemed like a good kind of mental exercise. And for once it paid off big. On my tenth pull-up, Lymie shadowboxed my face all the way up. Only this time he forgot about the bar, and when my face went behind it—Bam!—he slammed that thing so hard I could almost feel the doorway move.

"Aaaaaah!" he yelled, falling to the floor and rolling around. "Aaaaaah!" He couldn't even speak or swear or anything. He just rolled up in a ball with his fist in the middle and kept yelling "Aaaaaah!"

I waited for the yelling to die down, and then I knelt down next to him and said real gently and quietly, "It hurts to punch steel things, doesn't it, Lyme?" I patted him on the shoulder. "Maybe next time we'll remem—"

That's as far as I got. Lymie uncoiled like a rattlesnake or something, wrapped his arms around my head, twisted sideways until my face was on the floor, and cranked on the pressure for all he was worth. I don't know how I heard him with his arms locked around my ears the way they were, but I did. He was saying, "You think it's funny? You think it's funny?" But it wasn't like he wanted an answer or anything. Every time after he'd say it, he'd arch up and cram his body into my head a little harder and crank down on his arms a little harder till I thought my head would go flat. By now *I* was the one yelling "Aaaaaah!" I couldn't help it. I was in serious pain.

All of a sudden he stopped. Which could mean one of two things: He thought I'd learned my lesson (fat chance). Or Mom was standing there (more likely). I slipped out from under him and sat up. The lenses of my eyes were kind of too squished in to focus all the way, but there she was, with her arms folded and giving us that "can't I leave you two alone for two minutes" look like she always does.

"Do you have to fight every day?" she said wearily. "Will you ever grow up?"

I felt around my head to see if it was the right shape. "We were just fooling around," I said, trying to sound like I hadn't just about been killed.

"Well then, why don't we stop fooling around before something gets broken or somebody gets hurt?" She stared at us a second to make sure it'd sunk in.

As soon as she left, Lymie sat down next to me, patted me on the shoulder, and said as quietly and gently as can be, "It hurts to bust on Lymie, doesn't it, Ty?"

✧ IV ✧

ON MONDAY SOMETHING happened. I mean, things happen every day, but usually they don't amount to anything. But this was different. Something big happened and I was right there. And I mean *right* there.

It'd been a pretty quiet day. My body had spent all morning going through the routine of the school day, but my mind was busy feeling nervous because we'd be having our first wrestling practice that afternoon. Sunday night I had this nightmare where I'd been exercising for like two hours straight and I was about ready to pass out, and every time I'd let up for even a second the Coach would crack a whip two inches away from my head and yell, "PAIN IS THE NAME OF THE GAME, GIRLIE! GET USED TO IT!" It was only a dream, but I had this feeling that the real practice wouldn't be all that different.

Right before lunch, I was zipping down the stairs when all of a sudden I found myself behind Old Lady Waverly, my science teacher. I slammed on my brakes. Seeing how she was kind of fat for one thing, and kind of old for another, she was moving at about half a mile an hour. She'd lower one foot onto a step, then lower the other foot onto the same step, and then make sure everything was all right before doing the same thing on the next step. Which wasn't unusual. That's the way she always did stairs. But the thing was, the whole staircase was empty except for the two of us. My social studies teacher had sent me out ahead of the bell so I could deliver a note for him to the office. And now I didn't know what to do. I figured if I passed her she might start yelling at me for walking recklessly or something, and if I stayed behind her I'd look like an idiot going half a mile an hour down the whole flight of stairs. Plus, if I did that, she might even think I was being a wise guy and start yelling at me anyway.

So I bent over and pretended to be tying my shoe until I could decide on a plan. I was about to stand back up, pretend like I'd forgotten something, and hang a U-turn, when it happened. First I heard this sound come out of her. It was...I don't know...something between a squeak and a gasp maybe...not the kind of sound you'd expect to come out of somebody as big as Old Lady Waverly, especially if you knew her, which I did. And right after this squeaky gasp, she seemed to kind of stiffen up for a second, like the railing she was holding had electricity running through it. Then she kind of crumpled up right in front of me. She did it pretty slow, like an inflatable doll or something losing air, only she didn't get any smaller. The next thing I knew she was stretched out across the stairs. I ran toward her because I knew she'd start to roll, but I was too late. She flopped down to the landing. And two seconds later I was crouched right beside her.

"Hey, Mrs. Waverly, are you all right?" I asked her, even though a moron could tell she wasn't. She was looking up at me, but she didn't seem to be focusing. And she was moaning like she was having a bad dream. Only she wasn't moving. At all.

I crouched down even lower, hoping she'd come to enough so she could whisper to me what to do. She didn't. She kept on with the moaning noises.

Suddenly the bell rang, and I could hear a million kids running out into the halls above me and below me. I looked down to the first floor. A bunch of kids came flying around the corner and started up the stairs. Then they saw me crouched down next to Old Lady Waverly and they all stopped. They stopped so fast it caused chain reaction collisions behind them. I looked up to the second floor. Same thing. There weren't any teachers there yet, and nobody knew what to do any better than I did.

All of a sudden I saw Lymie's head poking out from behind everybody else's on the second floor. He was all bug-eyed.

"Tyler," he said in a voice that sounded like he'd just seen a ghost. "What'd ya do to her?"

For the rest of the afternoon I kept thinking about Old Lady Waverly collapsing like that and rolling down the stairs. And it made me kind of depressed. Which was strange. Old Lady Waverly was my absolute meanest teacher. No contest. You'd think I'd want to pay money to see somebody that mean take a major tumble. Only it seemed to work just the opposite. Seeing her lying there all helpless and moaning really made me feel terrible. I felt so sorry for her I couldn't believe it. And the thing is, I think I felt *more* sorry for her because she *was* mean. If she'd've been nice or something, I still would've felt bad, but...I don't know...nice people are different. You never seem to feel as sorry for them. Like you know they're stronger and can face up to things better. Plus, the way I figure it, if you're a nice teacher and you're all crumpled up on the landing of the stairs in some school and everybody's gawking at you, you'd kind of know that everybody felt bad and was hoping you were all right and everything. But if you're some nasty old teacher that everybody hates, it'd be a whole different story. You'd figure that everybody was all happy about seeing you get paid back for all the rotten things you'd done to them. And even though Old Lady Waverly couldn't answer me or anything when I asked her if she was all right, there was something about the look in her eyes that made me feel like she knew everything that was going on. Her eyes were *scared.* I don't know what it is that makes eyes look scared, and I actually only looked into them for a second, but that was enough. And every time I thought about Old Lady Waverly lying there, I'd see those scared eyes again.

Pretty soon after the bell rang, some teachers must've found out what happened because they came running and blocked off traffic (which didn't need to be blocked off that much since nobody was coming near us anyway). At first I didn't even think any teachers would come down—or up—to us, and I was really getting ready to panic. Then Mr. Bailey, my English teacher, ran up from the first floor. He crouched down next to me and started to prop up Old Lady Waverly's head.

"She just fell," I said in this voice that didn't sound like my own. "She was going along fine and then she fell."

"It's all right, Tyler," Mr. Bailey told me and tried to push me away. "You go to lunch. We'll take care of her."

By then the nurse was already crouched down next to us. She grabbed Old Lady Waverly's wrist and started taking her pulse.

"She just fell," I told her as I stood up. "I wasn't even that close to her."

"Go," she said, without even looking up. "We'll take care of her. Go!"

So I went down to the cafeteria. As soon as I sat down,

Lymie found me and wanted to know every detail about what happened. He was all excited.

"Wow," he kept going. "I don't believe it. I wish I coulda been there. I don't believe it."

"Shut up, Lymie," I told him every couple of minutes. Meanwhile he was shoving food into his face with both hands. I was picking at this salad that I got. I'm the only kid I know who ever gets a salad in the cafeteria. Lots of teachers (the skinny ones) get salads, but kids?...Never. But the only other thing on the menu I could eat (besides dessert) was the pizza, or at least this thing that comes out on a humongous tray and looks like it might be a member of the pizza family. One day I finally got up enough nerve to try it, and it wasn't bad. Only today my stomach was in knots, and I didn't think I could handle pizza.

Lymie got the more traditional school lunch: two cheeseburgers, fries, and two ice cream sandwiches. The kind of high fat, high cholesterol stuff the Coach wanted me to eat so I could put on weight and win wrestling matches even though I'd probably get a heart attack before the end of the season.

"So whaddaya think happened to her?" Lymie wanted to know.

"I don't know," I said. "I think she just passed out. It was right before lunch. Lotsa times I get light-headed right before lunch if I haven't eaten anything all morning."

"You're light-headed all the time," Lymie said. "Probably because there's nothing *in* your head."

This, in Lymie's book, is world class humor, and he cracked up and started slapping the table. I ignored him. With Lymie, sometimes fighting back just encourages him.

"So you think she'll be in school tomorrow?" Lymie said when he got done yukking it up.

"Probably," I said. "She'll probably even be teaching this afternoon. I don't think she hit her head or broke anything. She made a pretty soft landing."

This cracked Lymie up, and me too when I thought about it, because it made Old Lady Waverly sound like some kind of airplane. Lymie said if she *was* an airplane, she'd be one of those big, fat cargo planes they use in the army to fly jeeps and tanks and stuff around.

Just then Mary Grace Madigan and Babette Flosdorf sat down next to us, and they wanted to know what was so funny. So we told them about Old Lady Waverly and fat airplanes. Neither of them laughed. Or even smiled. Mary Grace doesn't believe in laughing at people and saying mean stuff. Babette does, but she's kind of fat herself.

"Sometimes you guys can be so immature," Mary Grace said.

"Not to mention sleazeball slimes," Babette added.

Lymie and I looked at each other. And I don't know why, but we both cracked up for like five minutes straight. It didn't matter that I really did feel bad about Old Lady Waverly taking a fall, or that Mary Grace told us that if we couldn't act normal they were leaving, or that when they got up to leave Babette punched me really hard in the arm. In fact, all those things made me crack up even more.

Old Lady Waverly didn't make it to seventh-period earth science class. They pulled some other teacher in to watch us. Which meant study hall since no other teacher in the school cares about rocks. Some of the kids said how they had taken her away in an ambulance. I figured that was pretty normal procedure. When somebody that old passes out and falls down the stairs, they'd probably want to take her in and check her out and keep her there the rest of the day for observation. To make sure there were no internal injuries or that kind of thing.

Mary Grace poked me between the shoulder blades. "You still think it's funny?" she said.

"I never said it was funny, Mary Grace. We were just laughing."

"Oh, that makes a lot of sense," she said.

I didn't even try to explain. She was a girl. It'd be like trying to explain to my mother why Lymie and I crack up so hard over the Three Stooges. Like Moe will slap Larry across the face or rake a saw across Curly's head and my mother won't even crack a smile. And she always has to say, "Now I'd like to know what's funny about that?" And if you try to explain it, you end up looking like a jerk.

"Forget it, Mary Grace," I told her. "It's beyond your comprehension." And I said it really smug like I was talking to a little kid or something.

✧ V ✧

THE FIRST THING we did at wrestling practice was to go out and run up and down the stairs fifty times. I thought the Coach would start practice by making some big speech or something to make sure our attitudes got started on the right foot. But his big speech turned out to be "FIFTY...UP AND DOWN."

Everybody took off for the stairs, so Lymie and I did too. I was pretty happy for myself because running is my thing and I could probably run up and down stairs all day. But I felt sorry for Lymie. He was all decked out in this big sweat suit because he figured it'd help him lose weight. I told him that a sweat suit doesn't help you lose real weight, only water. He told me to shut up. Lymie doesn't like to have his thought process interfered with by scientific facts.

We all started running up and down the stairs in single file, two and a half flights one way, because the school's two stories tall and the gym and the band room are like half a story below the main floor. You had to be careful not to run into any teachers or kids staying after school, especially on the first floor where you had to cross the main hallway to get to the little flight to the gym and the band room. And you couldn't stop and look both ways or anything because the Coach was right there at the bottom yelling things like "KEEP UP THAT PACE! WHAT DO I GOT HERE, THE GIRLS' FIELD HOCKEY TEAM? KEEP IT MOVING!" And sometimes you'd see one of the women teachers, usually one of the younger ones who didn't believe in men saying nasty things about girls, stop and look at him like he was some kind of boob. Which, even though I was only thirteen, I already knew.

We were moving right along, and by about the fifth lap Lymie was already huffing and puffing something fierce. I was afraid that before he got anywhere near fifty done, he'd pass out or throw up or something. So on the next flight up I pulled up next to him and told him that if things got too bad, he should stay on the top floor every other lap so he could catch his breath. There were probably fifteen or twenty of us and we were all spread out in a pretty steady stream, so chances were pretty good the Coach wouldn't notice one less kid every other lap. Plus I figured the Coach couldn't count that high anyway without taking off his shoes and socks. Lymie shook his head and poured on more steam. You had to kind of admire the guy.

Lymie was hardly even done shaking his head when this kid ahead of us, Victor Grouse, turned around and kind of hissed at Lymie through his teeth, "Don't even think about stopping, chubs, 'cause I'll be watching."

Victor was one of the co-captains of the team, along with Ox, but unlike Ox, Victor was not a nice guy. He had a body that looked like it had been chiseled out of granite. Even his face had these rippling muscles, especially when it was angry, which it usually was. And his angular crew cut didn't add any to his charm.

"He didn't say anything," I said, even though I was pretty scared of Victor, because Lymie's getting yelled at was my fault.

"I know," Victor said. "You did." He gave me a quick "I'll be watching you" kind of glare over his shoulder before turning around again.

"Fascist," I whispered to Lymie, hoping Victor wouldn't hear me.

"Shut up," Lymie told me. "You're gonna get us in more trouble."

I sighed and dropped back into single file. It looked like it was going to be a long season.

After our last lap, we ran through the gym, where the varsity basketball team was practicing, and up the steps onto the stage, which was where the wrestling team got to practice. The stage separated the gym from the auditorium, and with the curtains drawn on both sides it was a dingy, claustrophobic room with absolutely no natural light whatsoever. There could be a major hurricane or blizzard or something going on outside, and you'd never know it from up on that stage. The stage curtains were so thick that even the basketball sounds from the other side were muffled. I stood there thinking what it would be like spending every day after school for the next three months in that dungeon with the Coach.

"TWEET!"

I just about jumped out of my sneakers. I turned around. The Coach was standing right behind me with this whistle on a rope dropping out of his mouth.

"MAT!" he yelled.

When I looked around to see who Matt was, I noticed everybody else—even Lymie—was starting to unroll this humongous green mat across the stage.

"YOU HARDA HEARING, McALLISTER?" the Coach said to me. "MAT!"

I ran over and started pushing on the mat too. No sooner was it all unrolled than he grabbed the whistle again.

"TWEET!"

Even though I saw it coming this time, I still kind of flinched. A whistle's one thing when you're out on an athletic field, or even when you're spread out around a gymnasium, but when you're all standing around on some little stage, it's a whole different story. It seems to cut right through your brain.

"DROP AND GIVE ME FIFTY!" the Coach yelled, and everybody spread out and started doing push-ups. Every once in a while the Coach would see something that made him mad and he'd tweet his whistle at some kid, then bend over and start screaming something into the kid's ear like "GET THAT TAIL DOWN! I WANT THAT BACK STRAIGHT!" Or "OFF THAT STOMACH! A WRESTLER NEVER LETS UP!"

We all kept doing push-ups for all we were worth. And even though I'm on the thin side, when I got to thirty, I felt like I weighed five hundred pounds.

"TWEET!" That tweet was for me. When I cranked my head around, I saw the Coach glaring down at my face.

"WHAT ARE YOU, McALLISTER, SOME KINDA INCHWORM? LOOK AT YOURSELF!"

I looked. And I realized what he was all mad about—my shoulders were in the air, but my hips were still on the mat.

I took a deep breath and leveled myself off.

"NOW KEEP IT LEVEL! NONE OF THIS INCH-WORM STUFF!"

Mustering up all my strength, I managed about five more level push-ups before I heard the whistle go off on the other side of the stage. Then I went back to being an inchworm.

Next we did squat thrusts. Fifty. I started to wonder if maybe fifty was the only big number the Coach knew.

"EXTENSION! I WANNA SEE SOME EXTENSION!" he'd yell if he spotted somebody who wasn't thrusting enough.

Then we were supposed to roll around on our heads for a while. Right away I knew this wasn't good. At least not for somebody who planned on someday using his head for something other than rolling around on it. What we had to do was get on our backs and then keep arching up until all our weight was on our feet and our heads. And that was only the beginning. Then the Coach expected us to keep arching back until our heads bent around under our shoulders, and then to rock back and forth and from side to side. Which I thought was physically impossible until the Coach had Victor demonstrate. Within two seconds, Victor had plunked himself down on the mat, arched his back up, rolled his weight up onto his head, and backpedaled with his feet until his eyeballs were practically scraping vinyl. Then he started rocking, first rolling from his forehead to the top of his head and back, and then twisting sideways from one ear to the other. And for good measure he started running around in circles with his feet like some kind of drunken spider. The kid didn't have muscles in his neck; he had steel cables.

The first thing I noticed when I tried arching up onto my head was pain. Serious pain. Which was probably why the Coach liked that particular exercise so much. To start with, my neck wasn't crazy about supporting half my weight, and when I rolled myself back toward my forehead, I half expected to hear something snap. Plus the wrestling mat was not all that soft, and unlike my feet, which were made to be stood on, my head wasn't padded.

"ROLL BACK ON THOSE HEADS!" the Coach was yelling. "A WRESTLER'S GOTTA HAVE A STRONG NECK!"

I started to rock back and forth a little bit, and for a few seconds I forgot all about my twisted up neck and my unpadded head. That was because every time I moved at all in any direction, the mat felt like it was ripping the hair off my head. In one piece. Mr. Clean probably wrestled as a kid.

I could hear groaning sounds coming from all around me, so I knew I wasn't alone in my pain. One time right after the Coach yelled "ARCH IT!" I heard Lymie go "Aaaah!" and a few seconds later a Southern version of the same sound came out of Justin. Next I felt this hand come up under the small of my back and rock me further onto my forehead. The next "Aaaah!" was mine.

"WE'RE GONNA BUILD THOSE PENCIL NECKS UP! COME ON, LET'S KEEP MOVING SO WE CAN START GETTING COMFORTABLE ON THOSE HEADS!" Which was kind of like telling us we should get comfortable with the idea of holding our hands over an open flame. Or sleeping on a bed of nails. Two things that the Coach probably did in his spare time.

After about three minutes of learning to get comfortable on our heads, the Coach told us to get up and grab a partner for some mat work. I felt the top of my head, which was tingling like crazy, to make sure there was still hair on it, and then turned toward where Justin and Lymie were because they were the two kids closest to my size. I looked at Justin first because he was lighter than Lymie, and he shrugged at me and nodded. I started toward him, but before I'd even finished my first step, I felt this viselike grip on my arm. Turning around, I found myself face to face with Ox.

"Hey, partner," he said and started pulling me over to his corner of the mat.

"OX! WHAT DO YOU THINK YOU'RE DOING?" The Coach came over and stuck his face in Ox's face.

Ox shrugged. "You told us to get a partner, Coach. I got John Henry here."

The Coach just stood there for a minute. He looked like he might be getting ready to foam at the mouth or something. Then he thought up what it was he wanted to say.

"GET A REAL PARTNER, OX! A REAL PARTNER!" He turned to me. "You! Get with him," he told me and jerked his thumb toward Justin.

I ran over to where Justin was, kind of relieved, and we spent most of the rest of the practice working on escapes from referee's position. That's where one kid gets on his hands and knees, and the other kid crouches down next to him and wraps his right arm around the first kid's stomach and puts his left hand on the kid's elbow. Only you couldn't just get into position and relax until you heard the whistle. If you were on top (that's offensive position), you were supposed to grab the other kid and hold him with "real authority" as the Coach put it. And if you were on the bottom (that's defensive position), you had to make your whole body like a coiled spring and dig your fingers into the mat, which was almost impossible unless you happened to be born with claws. The Coach showed us three different escapes from the bottom, and then we had to take turns practicing them. Justin and I got yelled at quite a bit because it seemed that no matter what he showed us, we'd still end up flopping around the mat the same old way. Plus sometimes he'd catch one of us not being a coiled spring or not holding the other kid with enough authority, and he'd start screaming about that. If it wasn't for Lymie and his partner, Jake Kiley, who also never wrestled before, the Coach would have been able to pull up a chair and spend the entire time bellowing instructions at Justin and me and then groaning when we actually tried to do what he said. Only every few minutes he'd have to run over and bellow at Lymie and Jake about something stupid they were doing, so we'd get at least a little break.

Still it came as kind of a relief when Ox and Victor got up in front to lead us through calisthenics—even though it wasn't like gym class where you could stop and catch your breath whenever the teacher wasn't looking. Victor watched all of us like a hawk (especially Lymie and me, I thought) and the Coach paced around behind us just waiting for somebody to let up so he could blast their eardrums. By the time we got done, my whole body felt like soft rubber, and my head felt like it was floating about two feet above my shoulders.

But in some strange way I felt good. I'd made it through the first practice.

Lymie took the late bus home, and I walked most of the way to my house with Justin, who it turned out lived only a couple of streets down from me. Which was good because if one of us collapsed under a bush or something, the other one could get help before he froze to death. We were almost halfway home before either of us had enough strength to even talk.

"You think that guy" (only he said 'gah') "knows how to coach?" Justin wanted to know. "Or is he bonkers?"

"I don't know," I said. "Maybe both."

We trudged on for a few more minutes.

"So where'd you come from?" I asked him. Justin had only been in Wakefield for about a month. It was obvious he was from the South, but I wondered where exactly.

"South Carolina," he said. "Columbia. But we lived in

Atlanta for the last two years." Every time he said something he'd raise his voice at the end, making it sound like a question.

"So how'd you end up here?" I said. "In Wakefield."

"My mom grew up around here," he told me. "My grandfather used to have a farm right outside town, only now he's retired and sold it." It took me a few seconds to figure out what he meant because he pronounced "retired" like "retarred."

"Okay," I said, "so your family came back to be with your grandfather?" I hoped I wasn't being nosy, but I was always curious about people and how they wound up in certain places and all that. Like if it was destiny or chance or what.

"Just me and my mom," he said. "My parents just got a divorce." He even made the divorce sound like a question. "How about you? Didn't somebody tell me your mom was Linda LaMar?"

"Yeah," I said. "She still goes by her maiden name, so that's why her name is different from mine. We only moved here last summer."

"How come? She's a famous actress. How'd she decide to move to Wakefield?"

I shrugged. "My mom lived around here when she was young too. In Saratoga. We lived in Los Angeles, but she thought she'd like to come back here." I didn't have the energy to tell him about my father being killed or my allergies or any of the other problems I'd had back there.

We split up when we got to Justin's street.

"Get rested up for tomorrow," he told me. "I think that gah is bonkers."

I expected Mom to yell because I'd walked home with wet hair, and when she didn't I should have figured something was up. And I thought Mom and Mrs. Saunders were looking at me funny when I sat down to dinner, but I figured they were just all worried because I looked worn out. Then when we started eating, Mom told me that the nurse had called right after school about Old Lady Waverly.

"Why?" I asked, puzzled. "I didn't knock her down. She just passed out or something."

"I know, hon," Mom said and put her hand on my hand. "But she didn't just pass out. She had a stroke."

"A stroke?" I said. "Is she...is she gonna be..."

"She died, hon. She died on the way to the hospital. There was nothing anybody could do."

I just looked at her. I didn't say anything. Whenever I hear about somebody I know dying, even somebody I'm not crazy about, it always feels like I've been punched hard in the stomach.

"The nurse was worried you'd be upset," Mrs. Saunders said, "since you're the one who found her. It was nice of her to call."

"Yeah," I said. And that was all I could say.

That night when I went to bed, I got to thinking about dying. About what it would be like. The whole idea of dying seemed so strange to me, even though I'd almost done it a couple of times. I used to get these really bad asthma attacks where I couldn't breathe. At first I'd panic and start fighting for air like some kind of crazy person, and pretty soon I'd pass out. But even after I passed out, I'd be a little aware of things like doctors working on me and giving me shots and oxygen and everything. I wondered if dying for real would be like that, only you'd black out completely and not be aware of anything. Like—poof—your body's still there but you're not. I didn't think so. I just couldn't imagine ever being gone like that. It didn't seem to me that you could be something one minute and then nothing the next.

I remembered reading this article once about these people who died and then were brought back to life. And the thing was, they all kind of said the same thing about it. After they died, they'd find themselves out of their bodies and looking down on the operating table or the scene of the accident or whatever, and at first they'd be a little surprised to see it was them who was lying there. Then they'd usually hover there for a while and watch the doctors or ambulance guys or whoever and listen to what everybody was saying. And while everybody else'd be all panicky (the live people), the dead people would feel pretty good, and they'd start to wonder what all the fuss was about. After a while, the dead people would find themselves going through this...I don't know...kind of a tunnel or something, and they'd see this light up ahead. And sometimes the light would have some religious person like Jesus or Buddha in it, and sometimes it'd have their dead relatives who'd be there to welcome them. But that's as far as anybody got. Everybody in the article got brought back to life before they really got the whole story, so what would've happened to them next is anybody's guess. But except for people who'd tried to kill themselves, they all thought dying had been a pretty great experience. The article told about one lady who cried for like a week after she woke up because she said the afterlife was so beautiful and peaceful that it made the regular world seem almost dingy and depressing.

Thinking about that lady reminded me of what Lymie's father told us one time about trying to get calves out of the barn in the spring after they'd been cooped up inside all winter. He said you'd get them as far as the doorway, and then they'd plant their feet and just stand there because they were afraid to go outside, and you almost had to belt them over the head just to get them out the door. But once they got outside and started to get used to the whole idea, they'd start running around and jumping up and down and everything like they couldn't believe how great it was to have a whole field to play in and fresh air and sunshine.

And I wondered if dying might be like that.

And I wondered about Mrs. Waverly (it didn't feel right calling her Old Lady Waverly anymore), and if maybe she'd been hovering around watching while I'd been crouched down beside her.

And I wondered about my father, and if he knew I was on the wrestling team and what he thought about it.

And I wondered if they were both happy now like Lymie's father's calves.

✧ VI ✧

THEY DIDN'T CANCEL school or anything on Tuesday. But it wasn't exactly business as usual either. They had the flag in front of the school lowered to half-mast, and they turned part of the library into what they called a crisis intervention center, which is something they must've thought up after BooBoo Anderson, one of the janitors, drowned at the beginning of the school year. The way it worked was, if you got really depressed about Mrs. Waverly dying, say during math, you could get right up and go to the library to be counseled about it. Legally—you wouldn't even be marked absent. Plus they had other counselors (mostly teachers who had subs covering their classes) stuck around different parts of the school in case anybody needed them. That last part seemed pretty farfetched because even if somebody did feel bad about the whole thing, he still ought to be able to make it up to the library without needing counseling on the way.

At the beginning of my first-period class, the social worker, Mr. Chirillo (who liked being called Bob), came marching down the hall with this gang of kids that looked like they might have been picked up in a police raid or something. Right in front of our doorway he stopped and lowered his face into this walkie-talkie he was carrying like some kind of platoon commander. "I've got that group from the shop area," he said. "We're heading for the library. Over." His walkie-talkie squawked some kind of answer I couldn't make out, and he took off after the kids who had already left him in their dust.

Our English teacher, Mr. Bailey, stopped writing stuff on the board and waited till the hall got quiet again. "I do hope he's able to work them past their grief," he said.

We all laughed. Most of the kids on their way to be counseled were the regulars from Buster's Game Room who spent all their out-of-school time hanging out smoking cigarettes and swearing and looking tough, which was pretty much the way they tried to spend their in-school time, only usually they got chased to class, not to some crisis intervention center.

"That's so fake," George Rafferty said. "They're just using Mrs. Waverly as an excuse to get out of class."

Mr. Bailey looked at George and kind of thought for a minute and then looked around at the rest of us. "You all agree?"

We all did—at least about the kids who had just gone by. But Mary Grace raised her hand and said she'd seen a couple of kids that morning who'd really been crying. She thought they might actually need some counseling.

"Yeah," George said. "Girls. They'd be crying if they heard about a dead fly."

"Watch it, pal," Babette Flosdorf said from across the aisle.

"Yeah, well they were probably faking anyway," George said.

Then some of the kids wanted to know what Mr. Bailey thought.

"Well," he said, shrugging, "it seems to me you're discussing two separate issues. The first is whether some of the emotions we've seen displayed this morning are genuine and whether some of the students are taking advantage of the situation. I can't answer that question, although I hope all of us do have some genuine feelings of sorrow about losing Mrs. Waverly." He came around and leaned on the front of his desk. "I know many of you may have thought Mrs. Waverly was a little too strict, and a little old-fashioned maybe, but I knew her. She was a good woman and she cared about her students. She really did." He paused for a few seconds to let that sink in. "The second question is this: Assuming there are students in school who are genuinely grieving, does that mean they need professional counseling? What do you say to that?"

We argued about that for a while. Most of the kids thought that the idea of a crisis intervention center being set up because somebody died was kind of a joke since *everybody* was going to die sooner or later. But a few kids like Mary Grace thought it was good to have professionals to help people sort through their emotions. Then Mr. Bailey told us how death used to be a lot more a part of life than it is now, and how if you go to an old cemetery, you'll see tons of graves for kids since half of them never even made it to adulthood because of diseases and things. Plus people used to die more in their homes, and now dying people are more likely to be sent off to some hospital or nursing home. And he suggested that maybe we've forgotten that death is a natural part of life.

I thought about that for the rest of the period. About what it would be like having only a fifty-fifty chance of becoming an adult, and even if you made it, how you'd've lost half your friends. And I thought how people back then must've been different, the same way I was different after my father died, only more because they'd've been through that kind of thing over and over. Only I didn't quite know how they'd be different because I couldn't even put my finger on how I was different now, even though I knew I was.

During third-period study hall, I went to the library. Partly to get a book, and partly to see what was going on. I plunked my pass on the librarian's desk.

"Counseling or library work?" the librarian said, like she was really bored. Maybe even a little disgusted.

"Library work," I told her. She twitched her head to the left. "Stay on that side. If you need anything from reference or nonfiction, I'll get it for you. That's now our crisis intervention center." She said "crisis intervention center" extra slow like she was talking to a foreigner or something.

I went over and started browsing through fiction, but my eyes kept wanting to look at the action on the other side. About thirty kids, mostly girls, were over there. The only boys were the police-raid-looking kids that'd been hauled in earlier. A few of the girls were crying, and every once in a while a couple of them would hug each other, but most of them were just sitting around. Some of them had chips and soda, and you could tell that really bugged the librarian. Ordinarily no one was able to haul so much as a crumb or a drop of anything into there. I noticed a couple of girls who'd give the librarian this smug half-smile every time they took a swig or a bite of something.

"I'm here to tell you," Mr. Chirillo (Bob) was saying, "that it's all right to be upset. Hey, somebody died. Being upset's normal. That's what I'm here for." He looked everybody over. "So let's keep going. Let's get our feelings out in the open."

It was quiet for a few seconds. Then I heard this humongous snuff.

“I talked to her just last week.” It was the girl who had snuffed and now she was crying full throttle. She was exactly the kind of girl that bugged Mrs. Waverly the most. You know—pretty, popular, kind of wise. She snuffed again and continued. “She told me to get to class. I thought she was mean at the time, but now I see that she just cared enough to want us to do well.” This set her off again, and a few others joined in.

“So how do you feel about that?” Mr. Chirillo said, pacing between the tables. “How do you feel about the fact that you thought she was mean and now she’s gone? Let’s talk about that.”

I decided I’d heard enough to last me a while and headed for the librarian’s desk to get my pass.

“You don’t like our little show?” she asked me.

I shook my head. “I hope I never die around a school,” I told her and then looked up at her, afraid she might yell at me for being wise.

“Come back and see us when we’re a library again,” she said, and she gave me the first smile I’d ever seen her give.

So the whole day was pretty strange. Some of the boys were laughing and acting like the whole idea of Mrs. Waverly dying was a joke, which seemed kind of mean, and some of the girls were hugging each other and crying, which seemed kind of phony. But the strangest thing was that no matter how hard I watched everybody I couldn’t figure out what they thought about the whole thing. They joked or cried or whatever, but I had the feeling that all that stuff was just on the surface and most of them were only doing whatever they thought they were expected to do—you know, the girls being sensitive and the boys being wise. I don’t even know if any of *them* knew what they really thought.

At lunch the conversation started to get a little more normal, and everybody (all the guys) started talking about who we were going to get for our new eighth-grade science teacher. For the morning classes they'd had regular teachers filling in again.

"I heard they were gonna ask Miss Williams to take the job," Lymie said. Then he poked me. "She's a real babe, Ty."

Over the last month or so I'd noticed Lymie starting to use words like "babe," especially if we were around the other guys. I didn't know if it was because he was getting older or because his family just got cable.

Sher, whose real name was Tommy Sheridan, gave a low dirty-sounding chuckle. "I could handle that," he said, nodding.

I'd heard all sorts of stories about Miss Williams, who'd been a student teacher when Lymie and everybody were in seventh grade. Which was before I'd moved here so I'd never seen her.

"Why would she want to come here?" Jason Peters said. "She's got a job with the State already."

"Yeah," Lymie said, "but maybe she's tired of driving to Albany and back every day. Besides, who else are they gonna get around here who's qualified to teach science?" He turned to me. "I'm telling you, Ty. Hubba hubba!"

"Hubba hubba?" I said. "Can somebody check a calendar? I think I just entered a time warp."

"He's right though," Jason said. "She's a certifiable babe. Wait'll you see her and try to tell me she's not."

"She's hot," Sher said. "Very hot."

I knew the next thing that would happen was Sher would have to tell his shirt-tucking story, which even though I'd only been here for six months I already knew by heart. I think everybody else knew what was coming too. They all started eating and didn't say anything.

"Remember that day when she tucked my shirt in for me?" Sher started and didn't even seem to notice all the groans. "Boy, I'm telling you. I couldn't believe it."

I could feel his eyes zeroing in on me. Since I was the newest kid, whenever anybody had a story about seventh grade or something it always got directed at me, which kept up even after I'd heard everything about a million times.

"Listen, Ty," he said, jabbing me in the arm. "Miss Williams has this thing about shirttails. I come through the door, and she's up at the board writing. When she turns around and sees me, she goes, 'I'm not telling you again, Thomas. In my class shirttails stay in.' And then before I know what's happening, before I even set my books down, she runs over and starts doing it for me. She starts tucking in my shirt."

"You know it's funny how I don't remember that," Lymie said. "You sure it didn't happen in one of your dreams or something?"

"Hey, it happened all right and you know it," Sher said. "And I'll tell you something else. By the time she got done I was ready, man. I was red-dee."

"I bet she was too," Jason said. "Ready to throw up."

We were dying. Jason's pretty quiet most of the time, but sometimes he has this sense of humor like you wouldn't believe. We all started clapping him on the back and telling him, "Good one, Jase! Good one."

We knew Sher'd have to go for a comeback, so we braced ourselves.

"Yeah, well she wouldn't tuck in you guys' shirttails because she wouldn't wanna touch ya."

We all groaned. Sher's all right, but he's not that great in the wit department. Then I don't know who got it going, but we all started chanting "Red-dee, red-dee" and finished up with some barfing noises.

"Hey, laugh if you want," Sher said, "but you know it happened."

"Sher," Lymie said, "when you get to be a hundred years old, you're gonna still be telling that stupid story. Only by then you'll have her dressing you completely."

"Let him live with his memories, Lyme," Jason said, "'cause he wouldn't know what to do with it if he got it."

Just then Andrea Pratt and Jason's sister Christine plunked their trays down across from us. They were both in the ninth grade.

"Got what?" Andrea said.

We all looked at each other. And before we knew it we were all cracking up, same as yesterday at lunch. Andrea and Christine looked at us like we had two heads or something. And we couldn't've stopped laughing if our lives depended on it.

Seventh period I had science. I was the first one there for a change because I'd brought all my afternoon books with me to the cafeteria, and I didn't need to go to my locker or anything. I walked in expecting to see some teacher who'd wait for everybody to arrive and then tell us to shut up and find something to do. Plunking my books down on my desk, I looked up at the board to see if maybe there was an assignment. Instead I saw the back of this red dress. And this dress was seriously red. The lady in it was writing on the board. In perfect cursive letters she wrote "Miss Williams." Then she turned around and spotted me. "Oh, my first customer," she said and gave me this big smile.

I just stood there. I don't even think I smiled or anything.

And my eyes probably looked liked saucers. I couldn't believe it. She was gorgeous. And I'm not always running around saying stuff like that. I've hung around enough movie sets with Mom and my brother to have seen my share of good-looking women, and this one could hold her own around any of them. She had this long, silky auburn hair and these sleepy eyes that seemed like they were looking at you from some other world. I don't remember sitting down, but when Miss Williams turned to put the chalk in the tray, I noticed I was in my seat. I forced myself to blink a couple of times because I thought my eyeballs might be drying out.

Before I knew it the whole room was filled up with kids, and Miss Williams started in on attendance. We were all sitting in alphabetical order, so she just went down the list calling everybody's name and saying how good it was to see everyone again and all that. By the time she got to my name, my heart was beating something fierce and I was trying as hard as I could to look normal.

"And you must be Tyler McAllister." She pronounced my name softly—gently, like she was cradling it on some goose-down pillow or something.

"Yeah," I said and sat up straighter.

"You must be new," she said, "because I know I'd never forget those blue eyes."

I gulped. "Yeah," I said again. I could hear a couple of kids giggle.

"Well, welcome," she said. "Having my own class is rather new for me too, so we'll have to look out for each other, won't we?"

I think I nodded, but I'm not sure. Before I had time to worry about it, she was saying how nice it was to see Mary Grace and how she expected great things from her again this year. Which she'd probably get, knowing Mary Grace.

For the rest of the period my eyes were locked on Miss Williams. First she made a little speech about how sorry she was that Mrs. Waverly died, and that she would do her very best to see that we'd have a successful year and learn a lot about earth science and everything, and that she hoped we'd all get behind her and cooperate and help her do the best job she could. Then instead of telling us to open our books or putting notes on the board or something, she started telling us how you could tell the whole geological history of an area by going around and studying its rocks and how they're layered and what rocks are sitting next to what rocks. And then she told us about the glacier that came through New York about a million years ago, and how it gouged out the surface of the land and knocked down trees and everything and dropped tree trunks and rocks all over the place when it receded.

Winnie Fenwick wanted to know if the glacier knocked down people's houses, and Miss Williams explained that although our early ancestors probably did make their first appearance during this era, they wouldn't have had houses the way people do now. It sounded so good the way she answered Winnie's question, I kind of wished I could think of a question to ask her. Only I'm not in the habit of asking questions in class because it usually turns out the teacher has already explained whatever it is I'm asking, and I end up getting yelled at. I knew that wouldn't happen this time, since I hadn't missed a word, but I was afraid something else might go wrong so I just sat there.

The last thing Miss Williams told us about was how she'd like to arrange some field trips for next spring so we could go out and see for ourselves some of the things she was telling us about. Which I thought was a great idea. And not only because it would get us out of school—which is why most field trips are a good idea—but because I pictured myself on some perfect spring day walking around out in nature with Miss Williams telling us a story about every rock we came across.

When the bell rang it took me by surprise. That was a surprise in itself because I usually hear the clock tick all forty times in earth science. And when I left the room, I felt so good I couldn't believe it. In fact I felt so good I started feeling bad because Mrs. Waverly hadn't even been buried yet, and I figured if I had any decency I'd feel at least a little lousy. I tried to work up some sad thoughts about Mrs. Waverly, but every time I did I'd get this picture of that spring day, and I'd hear Miss Williams's hypnotic voice taking me back about a million years till it felt like I could almost sit on that glacier.

✧ VII ✧

I DIDN'T TELL Lymie or anybody, but I was hoping that since the school was supposed to be going through some crisis, they'd cancel wrestling practice. For starters, my body wasn't up for it. From the workout we'd had on the first day, my arms ached, my stomach muscles ached...almost everything I had ached. I thought that as the day wore on, the aches would wear off. They didn't. If anything, they got worse. And second, my mind wasn't up for wrestling either. It just wanted to hang around and daydream about Miss Williams and our field trips, and I knew after the Coach opened his mouth once, that'd be the end of my daydreaming for a while.

All day I'd been waiting for the announcement saying they were canceling all the after-school activities. But it never came. Part of me knew it wouldn't have made any difference anyway. The Coach would never let a little thing like somebody dying interfere with his chance of winning the... whatever it is you win in wrestling. And you could be sure the Coach wouldn't have counselors or anything sitting on the edge of the mat in case one of us got depressed.

Coach started off practice by saying, "AFTER OUR LITTLE WARM-UP YESTERDAY, I HOPE ALL YOU GIRLS ARE READY FOR A REAL WORKOUT TODAY!"

We all groaned. (Except maybe Victor.) As we headed for the stairs again to do laps, I caught a glimpse of the Coach's face and did a double take. I was pretty sure what I'd seen. I can't describe it, but it was similar to something that might pass for a smile on a normal person's face. And as I ran by, I swear to God I heard him go, "Heh, heh."

Later in the practice I got my wish. Only not the way I'd planned it. We were doing mountain climbers (that's like running in place except your hands are down on the mat, so if you turned the floor sideways you'd look like you were scrambling up the side of a mountain), and the Coach got all mad because he said nobody was doing it right. Which was to be expected because after two days in a row of practice, most of us were so drained that our arms and legs stopped caring about what they were supposed to be doing and started going every which way. Anyway, the Coach decided it was time for a personal demonstration of mountain climber know-how—a professional one, so he didn't use Victor or Ox this time. He strutted to the middle of the mat himself, patted his potbelly, and gave us his best "you're pathetic" look.

"WATCH THIS CLOSE, GIRLS, 'CAUSE I'M ONLY GONNA SHOW YOU ONCE," he said and then plunked down on all fours with his butt up in the air. "I WANT TO SEE THOSE LEGS GO WIDE." He pulled one leg forward outside where his stomach was hanging so that it stuck out past his chest. "YOU SEE WHERE THAT IS?" Then he threw that leg back as his other leg came forward and stuck out past the other side of his chest. "I WANT TO SEE SOME EXTENSION!" we could hear him saying as he started climbing the mountain faster and faster. "NONE OF THIS TIPPY-TOEING THROUGH THE TULI—"

"LI" was the last real syllable any of us heard. Then he kind of made a gasping noise and froze in place with his left leg sticking out past his chest and his right leg extended behind him. Which was pretty scary to me because gasping and freezing in her tracks was exactly what Mrs. Waverly did before she rolled down the stairs.

We pretty much froze in whatever position we were in too, wondering if we should do anything. For a few seconds the Coach stayed as still as a statue, but then I started to be able to make out a slight movement. Barely. You could tell he was moving his right leg in toward his body, only watching that leg move was like watching the minute hand go around on a clock. After what seemed like forever, both his feet were together and his butt was sticking way up in the air. With his yellow sweat pants and sweat shirt he looked like a fat golden arch. All the while it took the Coach to go from a statue of a mountain climber to a fat golden arch he hadn't made a sound, but as soon as he stopped we all heard this "Ooooooo..." sound. Like the kind of sound a ghost or something would make.

Ox bent over the opposite way from where the Coach was facing and stuck his face down next to the Coach's face. "Hey, Coach," he said. "You all right?"

The Coach's face was almost purple from being upside down for so long, and it was frozen in this big grimace. That didn't change when Ox spoke to him, but I swear to God if eyes could talk his would've said "IDIOT!" Finally you could see a little activity around his lips, and after about thirty seconds we all heard "Daaah—ck—tooor." It was like he pronounced it one letter at a time, which I know you can't do, but that's what it seemed like.

I took off before I even knew it. By then I was pretty sure he was getting ready to drop dead, and I was completely sure I didn't want to be there when it happened. I don't think I actually thought either of these things. But I think they were what was making me run so fast. The nurse's office was locked, so I poured on the steam down the long straightaway toward the main office.

"We need a doctor!" I yelled as I skidded through the door. "Coach Robilatto is having a heart attack or something!"

Two secretaries looked up at me from behind their desks. Neither of them batted an eye. I think they'd both worked in a school long enough so they'd gotten to the point where nothing surprised them anymore. Finally one secretary turned to the other. "I'll call the rescue squad. You call Mr. Blumberg."

They both started dialing. Two seconds later, the door labeled "Principal" flew open and Mr. Blumberg came tearing out and shot past all of us on his way to the gym. I don't know why, but I took off after him. By the time we got back to the stage, I was afraid Mr. Blumberg might be getting ready to have some kind of attack too. He was wheezing something fierce and he just stood on the edge of the mat looking over at the Coach, with me gawking out from behind him. All the guys were still clustered around the Coach, and a couple of basketball coaches were bent over the way Ox had been, trying to talk to him. Mr. Blumberg wheezed a few more times before joining everybody in the center of the mat.

I backed down the steps to the gym and stood there for a while outside the entrance to the boys' locker room. I felt like taking a shower and going home, but all of a sudden I had this stupid fear that the Coach might all of a sudden snap out of it and figure I was just trying to weasel out of a practice.

"Whaddaya think is wrong with him, Tyler?"

I turned and saw Lymie coming out from the stage stairs. And right behind him was Justin.

"I don't know," I told him. "But he didn't look so hot."

"That gah," Justin said, "was about as purple as a gah can get."

The rest of the wrestlers came down the steps then, so probably Mr. Blumberg and the basketball coaches had told them to get lost. Some of them milled around by the stage door and some of them headed for the showers, which is what Justin and Lymie and I did. We were just getting dressed when Ox stuck his head into the locker room and announced that an ambulance had just pulled up outside. Justin and Lymie practically flew into the rest of their clothes.

"Come on, Tyler," Lymie said, poking me with his elbow. "Let's check it out." He took off out the door with his shoes flapping and his shirt still unbuttoned.

I just sat there.

"Hey, Tah," Justin said, meaning Ty, "you gonna miss this?" He was grabbing up the rest of his stuff.

I shrugged. "What's to see?"

"I wanna see if they get that gah straightened up or if they load 'im the way he is."

Then Justin was gone too.

I walked home alone. As I left the locker room and started down the sidewalk toward the parking lot, I could see the red lights flashing over by the other side of the auditorium. By the time I reached the bus garage, the ambulance was going down Division Street between the elementary school and the middle school. Pretty soon it came around the other side of the middle school, stopped at the stop sign, and hung a right and quick left toward Main Street which, going east, became the road that would take it all the way to the hospital in Cambridge. The fact that the ambulance stopped for a stop sign, and the fact that it didn't even have its siren going, seemed to me to be a bad omen. Like maybe they were too late again.

I walked home the long way, sticking to the street. Usually when it wasn't dark, which it wasn't yet, I cut across the cemetery behind our property. Not only did it save a few steps, but if you're in the right frame of mind, a cemetery's kind of a neat place to walk through—all peaceful and quiet, and you can read all the names on the old stones and wonder who everybody was and what they were like and what happened to them and everything. But I was in no mood then for being around dead people.

When I came through the door, Mrs. Saunders looked up kind of surprised from the coffee table she was dusting and asked me why I was home so early.

"Something happened to the Coach..." That's as far as I got, and I could hear my voice start to crack, and I could feel my eyes start to water up. It caught me completely off guard. I mean, I wasn't exactly a big fan of the Coach.

Mrs. Saunders came over and gave me a big hug. Then she smoothed the hair back out of my face and looked down at me. Neither of us said anything for a minute. Finally, I took a deep breath and started in again.

"I think he had a heart attack or something. He was showing us how to do this exercise and..." My voice cracked again. "I think I'll start my homework," I said and headed for the stairs.

I was lying on my bed with my social studies book across my chest when I heard this little knock at my door. It was Mom.

She came in and sat on the edge of my bed. I didn't look at her because I was afraid I'd cry, but I could feel her hand come down and rest on my shoulder.

"Are you trying to scare us out of our wits, honey?" she said.

"Whaddaya mean?" I looked up at her.

She rubbed my shoulder. "When my son comes home and announces that he's going straight to his room to start his homework...well, you can't blame us for starting to panic." She moved her hand to my forehead. "No fever," she said. "And you don't look delirious."

I smiled. "I'm not," I told her. "And if it makes you feel any better, I'm not really doing homework. I'm just kinda hanging around."

"Well, that's not like you either. You always seem to have some project or another going. In fact, I spend quite a bit of my time worrying about what you're up to, but this...?" She paused, and I could feel her studying me. "Do you want to tell me about your coach?"

"There's not much to tell," I said. "First he's bent over showing us something...then he's having some kind of attack." I stared at my social studies book. "They took him to the hospital." I looked at her. "When it first happened, all I could think was how he looked just like Mrs. Waverly did the last time I saw her. And now all I can think is that he's probably dead." I looked down, and I could feel my eyes watering again.

"Most people who go to the hospital don't die," Mom said.

"Everybody dies," I said, and right away I was sorry because I sounded like I was accusing her of something. "I'm sorry. But you know what I mean."

"I know," she said, and we both stayed quiet for a while. I was thinking about my father, who was killed last year in a plane crash. And BooBoo Anderson, who broke his neck on the diving board at school in September. And Mrs. Waverly... And now the Coach.

"It's like..." I started in, "it's like anybody can die. And every time you look at somebody...I don't know...every time you see somebody, that might be the last time." I sat up and looked at her. "So how are you supposed to...I don't know...enjoy being with anybody when they might end up being gone the next day? And you might end up being alone."

And that's what it came down to. I hadn't realized it until I heard myself say it. I was afraid of being left alone. Still. Like when I was little and used to have this recurring nightmare where I'd fall off the edge of the earth, and Mom and Dad and Christopher and Mrs. Saunders would all be looking down at me, and I could see them but I could never get back to where they were. And I remembered having that same feeling when my father sent me away to boarding school. And then again when he died. Now every time somebody died or got killed or something, I'd kind of get that same feeling all over again. Not that I wouldn't feel sorry for the dead person or the dead person's family or anything. I would. But always lurking behind *that* feeling would be that *other* feeling. The fear.

Mom kept quiet for a minute. Then she said, "Maybe knowing that things are always changing is good for us. Maybe it reminds us to make the most of each moment and keeps us from taking each other too much for granted."

"I guess," I said and lay back down on my bed. I thought about some of the things I might have said to my father if I knew he was going to die. And how I would've tried to have gotten to know BooBoo more. And maybe even said something nice to Mrs. Waverly.

"Maybe all of life's a lesson," Mom continued. "And it's always trying one way or another to pound information into our thick skulls." She rapped her fist on the side of her head.

That was a pretty typical Mom speech, but it did make me feel a little better. Just thinking that the universe might have some kind of intelligence seemed to make a difference. It really did.

We heard a noise, and when we looked up, we saw Mrs. Saunders standing in the doorway.

"I don't want to bother you," she said, "but I've been calling around to check and see how your coach is. Well, I finally got through to somebody who knew something and found out he's all right." She came in and sat on the other side of my bed. "It was his back, you know. A slipped disk." She looked over to Mom. "You remember, Linda, my brother always had that problem. He never knew when that back of his was going to act up next. It was an awful thing." She looked down at me. "I knew you were worried, sweetheart, so I wanted you to know that your coach is going to be all right."

I thanked her, and Mom told her how thoughtful she was. As she was going out the door, we could hear her saying, "A back can be an awful thing."

Mom gestured with her hand toward where Mrs. Saunders had been. "You see how much we have to appreciate, how lucky we are?"

I nodded. I knew she meant about us having Mrs. Saunders, but she might have also meant about the Coach being all right.

"And I don't think," Mom said as she got up, "that you ever have to worry about being alone." She stopped in the doorway and looked at me. "I think you'll always draw people to yourself. I really do."

"Because of my great personality?" I asked. "Or my good looks?"

She smiled. "Because of your deep sense of modesty." And cocking an eyebrow, she left.

That night I tried to picture myself as an adult, and I tried to decide what kind of people I might draw to myself. Only I didn't come up with much. Half the time I pictured this old version of myself belting Lymie, and the other half I pictured this old version of Lymie belting me.

Anthony! My goodness!

nthony! What the heck?

nthony! Why do you
always cover your
ead?

thony! Put your hood
down!

nthony! Why must you
vex me?

Thanks good

Job

✧ VIII ✧

On wednesday the flag was still at half-mast and the crisis intervention center was still in business, with pretty much the same kids going to the library to get counseled, and pretty much the same kids getting rounded up and dragged in from around school property. During morning announcements, Mr. Blumberg said how Mrs. Waverly's wake would be held that afternoon and evening, and how her funcral would be the next morning.

"You gonna go to the wake, Ty?" Lymie wanted to know at lunch.

I hadn't put a whole lot of thought into it until he asked me. The only wake I'd ever been to in my whole life was my father's, and my memory of that was pretty foggy. Right after I found out that my father died, I had a serious asthma attack. The doctors and everybody were afraid it might happen again, and they'd given me enough medication to turn even my descendants into zombies. I remember sitting off to the side and being dimly aware of a parade of faces going by on their way up to the casket, and every once in a while a face would come in close and I'd feel my knee being patted or my cheek being kissed and I'd hear some murmurs about how sorry everybody was. The whole thing seemed like a dream. A bad one. I don't think I'd want to remember anymore about it even if I could.

"Hey, are you in there?" Lymie rapped on my head.

I looked at him. "Yeah, I'm in here."

"So are you going or what?"

I shrugged. "I don't know."

"I think it'd be kinda neat to go. You ever been to one?"

I looked down at the table. "Only my father's."

I heard Lymie kind of gulp. "Sorry, man. I forgot," he said and gave a little rap to my arm. Even though Lymie was my best friend, there were certain things we never talked about and this was one of them. I never told him not to, but he seemed to know enough not to bring it up.

Next thing I knew Sher and Jason plunked down across from us.

"Hey," Jason said, "either of you guys going to that wake today?"

I wasn't supposed to see it, but Lymie poked him under the table and then kind of jerked his head toward me. I must look really pathetic without even knowing it. Jason started eating and didn't talk anymore about wakes. Even Sher kept quiet, and that's saying something.

Miss Williams looked better than ever that afternoon. She was wearing this burgundy sweater and a wool skirt, kind of a blue and maroon plaid one. She could have been a picture in the L.L. Bean fall catalog. I'd thought about her enough over the last twenty-four hours so that when I walked in and saw her in person, it kind of took me by surprise and for a second even took my breath away. Like when you accidentally all of a sudden come across some big celebrity or something.

"Oh, hello, Tyler," she said, looking up and seeing me there. "You're first *again.* I admire your punctuality." Then she went up to the board and started erasing.

I noticed right away that she'd remembered my name and the fact that I'd been the first kid to arrive for two days in a row. That made me feel pretty good. Plunking my books down, I grabbed an eraser and started erasing toward Miss Williams from the other side. When we both got to the last word, our erasers met and stopped for a second. I was suddenly aware that my nostrils were filled with this perfume smell, something light and natural like lavender. I looked up at her.

"Thank you, Tyler," she said, setting her eraser on the chalk tray and giving me this big smile. "We make a great team, don't we?"

"Yeah," I said. "We do." And then I scooted back to my seat because I had a pretty good idea that I looked like I'd just been gonged over the head with something. By then other kids were starting to file in, and they were saying the usual things like, "Hey, Miss Williams, we doing anything today?" and "Do we need paper?" and "We supposed to have our books today?" I noticed a couple of boys had their shirttails out, and it kind of made me mad because I knew why they were doing it. Plus I think part of me was afraid that Miss Williams would go over and start tucking them in, just like Sher said she did for him. I knew that was stupid because I didn't own her or anything, but I also knew if she tucked in some kid's shirt, it'd really bother me.

She didn't. And she didn't answer all the questions the kids fired at her. She looked around and smiled and waited for everybody to get in their seats and for the bell to ring before she started. And she didn't start by yelling "Shut up!" or anything like most teachers do when they have an afternoon class that's still almost deaf from having had lunch in the cafeteria. In fact, she used that same silky smooth voice she'd used the day before, and we all had to kind of lean forward in our seats to hear her.

"As I told you yesterday," she said, "and as most of you may remember from last year, I would like you to bring your textbooks to each and every class. We may not use them every day, but we should have them on hand in case we need to refer to them. And as for paper, as well as pens, I think most of us would agree that we should bring these basic supplies not only to science class but to all our classes."

"You didn't tell us about pens and paper yesterday," Ricky Stewart yelled from the back of the room. Ricky was the kind of kid who spent practically his whole day making sure his rights weren't being violated or anything. He'll probably end up being a lawyer.

Miss Williams didn't flinch. Very slowly her eyes traveled back to where Ricky was. "Well, Rick, now I have told you." She smiled and locked her gaze on him for a few seconds. Then when she figured she'd shut him up, she went back to talking to the whole class. "Another thing which I may not have mentioned yesterday is the little matter of shirttails." She looked around the room. "Certain shirts are meant to be tucked in, and certain shirts may be worn on the outside."

"How're we supposed to know which are which?" That was Ricky from the back again.

"That's a fair question, Rick," Miss Williams said and held her gaze on him again. "And I'll be glad to show you the difference. Would you stand up please?"

Ricky looked around for a few seconds, probably trying to

decide if a teacher had the right to ask a kid to stand up, and then he did it. He was one of the kids whose shirttails were out.

"And, Tyler," Miss Williams said, "would you be so kind as to stand up?"

My heart jumped up toward my throat when I heard my name. I was wearing a white polo shirt and I all of a sudden realized *it* wasn't tucked in either. As I stood up, I wondered if she meant for me to be another example of a slob or if I was supposed to look all right. I looked down at my shoes and waited.

"Rick," Miss Williams said, "your shirt has tails, and a gentleman always tucks tails in." She paused a second. "Now, notice Tyler's shirt—no tails—which means it may be worn in or out depending on your preference."

"What difference does it make?" Ricky said and kind of gave a little shrug.

Miss Williams smiled at him. "The difference is that in school we expect gentlemen to look like gentlemen, and in this classroom I not only expect it, I insist on it. Out there," she said, waving her hand toward the window, "you may look however you wish. In here you will try to look your best." She held her gaze on him again for a few seconds to make sure he didn't have another two cents' worth to add. "And now that we understand each other, I'm sure we won't need to have this discussion again. Now all of you with tails out, please go to the boys' room and tuck them in."

Two other kids got up and headed for the boys' room with Ricky. I figured when she had Sher's class earlier, there were probably about ten kids with tails out.

"Thank you, Tyler," Miss Williams said. "Thank you very much. You may sit down."

I sat. And I couldn't believe how good I felt. Usually when a teacher holds you up as a good example in front of the class, you feel kind of low, like a traitor to the other kids or a schoolie or something. But I didn't feel that way at all. I felt really good and kind of tingly all over.

The rest of the class went by the same as yesterday. I sat there and listened to every word Miss Williams said. I even took some notes. And when the bell rang, I almost jumped. It seemed like we were just getting started.

After class, Mary Grace asked me something about the Coach's bad back. I told her as much as I knew, which wasn't much, but when she started for the door, I kind of hung back.

"Well, aren't you coming?" she said. Meaning to our lockers, which we usually walked to together.

"I'll be right there," I told her. "I just have to do one thing." I stood there at my desk fumbling through one of my books, hoping Mary Grace wouldn't stand there and wait for me.

She hesitated for a second and then headed for the door. "If I don't see you before you leave, Ty, don't forget to bring your math book home."

I felt like a rat. Ever since I'd gotten to this school, Mary Grace had always looked out for me and made sure I wouldn't forget the stuff I'd need for classes or homework because, as my father used to say, I'd forget my head if it wasn't fastened on. And now I found myself trying to ditch her so I could be alone with some teacher.

Traitor! Schoolie!

Guilt feelings or not, no sooner was Mary Grace out of sight than I headed for the front of the room. I hadn't thought any of this out, so I didn't have any particular plan. And I wasn't alone anyway because Jill O'Brien was up there asking about homework or something. Which was probably just as well, since whenever I was around Miss Williams I couldn't remember how to talk if my life depended on it. So while the two of them were still talking, I grabbed an eraser and started erasing the board for all I was worth.

Just as I was finishing up on the board, I heard Jill thank Miss Williams and say good-bye. Suddenly I was aware that my heart was beating something fierce. I looked around to see if there was anything more I could find to erase.

"So how goes it in the science department?" That wasn't Miss Williams or Jill. Turning around, I saw Mrs. Beadle walking in. She taught seventh-grade English across the hall. So much for my plan, which I didn't have anyway. I let out this sigh of disappointment. (Or maybe it was relief; I couldn't tell.) I plunked the eraser down in the chalk tray and grabbed my books.

"Thanks, Tyler," Miss Williams said. "You're such a big help."

I nodded and tried to smile. "See you tomorrow."

Just as I was about to reach the door, I heard Mrs. Beadle go, "I see you have an assistant already."

And then I heard it. With my own ears. Just as I was stepping out the door and disappearing from their sight, I heard Miss Williams say, "Isn't he a doll?"

A doll. A doll! I couldn't believe it. She liked me too!

The next big surprise came right after I'd floated out into the hall and Mr. Blumberg got on the P.A. to make some closing announcements. Most of them were pretty routine stuff reminding everybody about after-school activities or meetings that'd been canceled or moved to another room or whatever. But then at the end he announced how the members of the wrestling team should report to practice as usual. Everybody, including myself, had figured we'd have at least a week off.

"I can't believe it," Lymie said, running up behind me in the hall. "They must've finally got the Coach straightened out."

But when we got to the boys' locker room and looked into the coaches' office, we didn't see the Coach—straightened out or otherwise. What we saw was Chuckie. Our very own Chuckie Deegan.

"Come on, guys," he said. "Get changed. We don't have all day."

Lymie and I looked at each other. And if it's possible, I think *my* jaw dropped down further than his.

✧ IX ✧

"LISTEN UP, GUYS," Chuckie told us after we'd all gotten changed and were sitting around him on the big wrestling mat. "Looks like Coach Robilatto is out for the season. He's having a disk removed from his back, and it'll be a while before he's up and around again."

I know that's the kind of news you're supposed to feel bad about, but all I felt was this little wave of relief. Just because I was glad the Coach hadn't died didn't mean I wanted to have him screaming in my face every afternoon. I still didn't know what Chuckie was doing there, but I figured that since Chuckie knew Coach Johnson, who's our gym teacher and also the athletic director, he'd asked Chuckie to fill in for a while till he could find a real coach.

"Okay," Chuckie continued, "we'll start practice with a ten-point drill. Then we'll spend some time working on basic take-downs and escapes. We want them to become a reflex. Next we'll wrestle, and then we'll finish with cals. Got it?"

Everybody got it. I'd been afraid at first that kids would try to fool around and give Chuckie a hard time like they do substitute teachers, but nobody did. Whenever Chuckie told us something, everybody listened so hard you could hear a pin drop.

"All right. So get into two lines on the side of the mat, and Victor and Ox will lead you through the ten-point drill."

As I was heading off toward where everybody else was going, I stopped next to Chuckie for a second.

"You ever wrestle before?" I said.

"Yeah, Ace. I've wrestled." And he gave me kind of a half smile and pushed me toward the side of the mat.

Chuckie did seem to know something about wrestling. Which I thought at the time he probably learned out of some book that afternoon. Like about the ten-point drill, which turned out to be this warm-up exercise consisting of a lot of different moves you might have to make as a wrestler. Chuckie didn't just watch us going through the drill; he'd stop us in the middle and show us stuff we were doing wrong.

The first exercise was kind of like a penguin walk, only you had to keep going up and down to strengthen your legs. Next we did these running forward rolls. Then a buddy-carry where your partner'd carry you one way and you'd carry him back. (I used Justin.) Then a wheelbarrow. Then a double-leg penetration drill. And on like that. It was kind of fun, like gym class when you're a little kid. We finished with fifteen stand-ups, where you had to spring to your feet and look like you were ready for action. When Victor demonstrated that one, he looked like something that might jump out from behind a bush at Yellowstone ready to attack some camper. But I kept my mouth shut, seeing how I didn't want to be the camper he was ready to attack.

As practice wore on, it started to dawn on me that Chuckie knew more about wrestling than he could've gotten out of any wrestling book. Which shouldn't have surprised me as much as it did. I already knew he'd earned black belts in judo and karate when he was in the service, and wrestling probably had a lot in common with both of them. Not only did he know how to do things, but he seemed to know what was going on around the mat all the time. Like if I was practicing some escape and I got to the point where I couldn't budge and was about to get pinned by Justin, I'd hear him yell something like "Lotta hips, Ace. Let's see a lotta hips." And if I still couldn't budge, I'd feel him pushing me through whatever move he wanted me to make. And he wasn't only doing that for me. At the same time he was pushing on me, I'd hear him yelling something like "Off your back, Lymie. A wrestler never spends time on his back."

Another good thing Chuckie did was he made sure none of the smaller guys got creamed by the bigger guys. With the Coach, if two humongous guys came flying through the air and landed on you, he'd yell, "KEEP ALERT, GIRLS! KEEP ALERT!" So I had already developed this habit of peeking out from under this tangle of our arms and legs to make sure we weren't about to get squished into the mat. Whenever Chuckie caught me doing that, he'd say, "Keep your mind on what you're doing, Ace. I'll watch the other guys for you." And he did too. Whenever somebody went to step on somebody else's head or started to go flying off the mat, it seemed like Chuckie was right there to intercept them, even if he was in the middle of explaining something to somebody else.

So all in all it was a pretty good practice. I learned some new things. I didn't get screamed at. I didn't get killed. But I did get a pretty decent workout. After calisthenics, I felt tired but not all rubbery-legged and bubble-headed like I had after the first practice. In fact, I even felt good.

Before we went into the locker room, Chuckie gave us this lecture about how wrestlers have to be just as light *off* their feet as they are on their feet. And then he showed us a few things we'd be working on over the next few weeks. First he did a back arch until his weight had rolled up onto his forehead, and he kept pushing till his nose was against the mat. Which was pretty much what we'd seen Victor do a few days earlier. But then Chuckie rolled over—only rolled doesn't quite do it because first he was backside down, and then—Bam!— he was backside up as quick as a snapped towel. A wet one. Next he kicked out of that position and his feet went sailing over his head until he was backside down again. Then he rolled over a bunch more times like he was wrestling an alligator or something; and just when I thought his head might start screwing into the mat, he popped up on his hands and feet and started doing this kind of kick-out drill where he'd throw a leg underneath as he'd shift his weight from one arm to the other, slapping the mat each time through like some kind of turbocharged break dancer. I hadn't even figured out how he did that when he kicked out with both feet, and next thing I knew he was standing there looking down at us. Of course, by now we were all staring at him bug-eyed and slack-jawed.

He smiled when he saw the looks on our faces. "You'll all be doing that in a couple of weeks," he said.

While we were getting dressed, all Lymie and Justin and I could talk about was how we couldn't wait to learn how to do those moves. If we didn't learn anything else for the whole season, we were going to make sure we ended up as light off our feet as Chuckie.

"I wonder where he learned to do that?" I said. "You think they were judo moves or something?"

"Don't you know who he is?" Victor butted in, sounding like it irritated him that anybody could be so dumb.

"Yeah, I know who he is," I told him. "He lives right next door to me." I didn't tell him how Chuckie was our groundskeeper because I figured he'd accuse me of being coach's pet or something.

"I know him too," Lymie said, maybe figuring that'd be a little insurance against Victor's lousy disposition.

"And you guys didn't even know he was state champion in his weight class for three years in a row when he was in high school?"

"I didn't live here then," I said.

"Me either," Justin said.

We all looked at Lymie, and he shrugged at us. Which didn't surprise me. Even though Lymie had lived in Wakefield his whole life, he still didn't usually know what was going on. Plus he would've been pretty little back then. Victor shook his head and started for the door. Lymie and Justin and I turned and looked through the big plate glass window of the coaches' office. Chuckie was fixing his hair in a mirror on the wall.

"Champion of the *state*," Justin said.

Lymie and I just nodded and stared some more.

Justin's grandfather, this huge guy in overalls and a big white beard, was waiting for him in a pickup truck in the parking lot. They offered to take me home, but I wanted to wait for Chuckie. There was a lot I wanted to ask him about. I climbed into his car and waited.

"Hey," I said to him before he was even all the way in the car, "how come you kept it a big secret about being a wrestling champion?"

"You never asked," he said as he started the car. "Besides, that was six years ago. Six years is a long time."

Neither of us said anything until we got to Main Street.

"I like the way you coach," I told him as we turned the corner. "That other guy...I don't know...I think he escaped from some maximum security place. He was always telling us how we should enjoy pain and everything."

Chuckie laughed. "Times change. Coaching styles change. He was my coach, you know, and he taught me a lot."

"Yeah?" I said. "You learned all that stuff you know from him?"

"Most of it," he said. "When I started out, I didn't know the first thing about wrestling."

"Me either." I thought for a minute. "Did you like him? I mean at the time. Or did you think he was crazy sometimes too?"

"Sometimes," he said.

"Which?" I asked. "Sometimes you liked him? Or sometimes you thought he was crazy?"

"Both," he said. "Any more questions?"

Chuckie and I are funny together. Chuckie's usually pretty quiet, and I usually am too; but when we're together I always come up with a zillion things I need to know. I think it's because since he always says as little as possible, I always wonder what's going on inside his head.

I looked at him. "Were you built like me when you started wrestling?"

"Huh?"

"Your build. Were you light like me? Or kinda chunky like Lymie? Or muscular like you are now? Or what?"

Chuckie pulled the car over and stopped. Which was strange

since we weren't home yet. I wondered if I'd finally worn him down and he was going to tell me to shut up or get out.

"I don't know," he said. "I was a little bigger than you maybe. But I was a freshman, so you're getting a head start on me. But I was built like you, I guess. What are you worried about? You'll do all right."

"Coach said I'll probably get ripped to shreds before Christmas."

Chuckie laughed. "He said that?" He thought for a second. "Nah, I give you till New Year's."

"Funny," I said and poked him. "Hey, what'd you stop for anyway?" I looked out the window and noticed we were parked across from the Cloud 9 Tavern. "We getting a pizza or something?"

Chuckie pointed up ahead. I looked down the street and saw a bunch of people milling around on the sidewalk. They were in front of Flavin's Funeral Home. I'd forgotten all about Mrs. Waverly's wake.

Chuckie clamped a hand on my shoulder. "You can wait here, Ace. I won't be long." Then he opened the door and started to get out.

"Wait," I said and grabbed his arm. "I'll go with you." But I didn't move. I sat there looking at him.

Chuckie settled back in his seat and studied me for a second. "You don't have to go, Ace. Why don't you stay here?" He looked me in the eye. "Look, you've seen more than your share of death in the last few years. You really have. And you don't know any of Mrs. Waverly's family anyway. So relax. I'll be back in a minute."

"No," I said. "I'll go. It's all right. Really."

And this time I opened the door and got out.

✧

Some guy in a black suit opened the door and let us in. I was following so close behind Chuckie that every time he slowed down or stopped or something, my nose would scrunch into his back. First we had to sign our names in the guest book or whatever they call it, and then the black-suited guy motioned for us to go down the hallway where there was a line of people trailing out of this room on the left. Chuckie headed for the line, and I was right on his heels.

I couldn't believe how many people had turned out for the wake. After a few minutes of waiting in line, we got close enough so if I peeked around Chuckie I could see into the room. It seemed practically jam-packed. There was a steady trickle of people coming out, and already there were about ten people behind us waiting to get in. It was strange to be surrounded by that many people and still have it be so quiet. You could hear a lot of murmuring in the background but no real conversations. So far I hadn't seen anybody crying.

A few minutes later we made it through the doorway. I peeked around Chuckie's side and saw that we were headed toward some kind of receiving line. I vaguely remembered Mom and Chris and my Aunt Catherine doing that during Dad's wake while I sat off to the side.

"Those are Mrs. Waverly's kids," Chuckie said, leaning his head down toward mine. "Three sons and a daughter."

The line moved forward some more. I peeked around and tried to get a glimpse of Mrs. Waverly's kids, but I couldn't really see them yet. The people ahead of us had gotten up to the first one, and I could hear mumbling back and forth, but I couldn't make out what anybody was saying. I stretched my head up as close to Chuckie's as I could. "Whaddaya supposed to say?"

He looked at me. "I don't know...You tell them you're sorry.

And if you want, you tell them who you are and how you happen to know their mother. That kind of thing."

The next time I peeked around, the line had kind of spread out enough so I could see her kids' faces. Only you couldn't call them kids really. They were older than my mother. And they all looked kind of like Mrs. Waverly—big heads, kind of thick around the jaw, and all with that same look that Mrs. Waverly had. I can't really explain it, but certain families have a certain look, and all these people had a Waverly look.

I was trying to memorize this little speech, telling them who I was, and how I was in Mrs. Waverly's class, and how I was sorry. When Chuckie got up to the first son, I was going over it one last time, and when he stopped to talk to the guy, I bashed my nose into him again. Into his shoulder this time. Chuckie wrapped his arm around my shoulder and made room for me in front of the guy. "And this is Tyler McAllister," he told him. "He was one of your mother's students this year."

I stood there. That was practically my whole speech. "Sorry," I said, and the way I said it, you'd think I'd stepped on his toe or something. He gave me a sad little smile and stuck his hand out for me to shake.

It went pretty much like that all down the line until we got to the daughter. When she looked down at me, you'd swear you were looking at Mrs. Waverly twenty or thirty years ago. I even kind of flinched just like I used to whenever Mrs. Waverly looked down at me.

"One of her students, you say?"

"Yeah," I said, and when she didn't say anything I added, "She was nice."

"Hmmph," she said. "She must have mellowed since I was in school. I don't remember any of the kids thinking Ma was nice back then." She peered down at me with her Waverly face.

"Well…bye," I said because I couldn't think of anything else. I started pushing into Chuckie to get him going. When we turned around, there we were—right at the foot of the casket. I'd been so nervous about going through the receiving line that I'd forgotten about the casket. We walked up to the front, the open part. My father had been a Catholic—sort of—so I knew about kneeling and everything, and Chuckie was still a Catholic—sort of—so we both knew what to do. Sort of. We plunked our knees on the kneeler facing the casket and started looking at Mrs. Waverly. At least I did. Maybe Chuckie was praying. I always wondered about that—how many people actually prayed when they kneeled down. That's another thing I'd have to ask Chuckie.

I wasn't shocked or anything when I saw Mrs. Waverly. She looked about the same as she always had, except she was wearing a better dress than usual—a dark blue one with ruffles—and a ton of makeup. Only not makeup like a movie star or a model would wear. This stuff was more powdery. The only other thing I noticed about Mrs. Waverly was how blank her face looked. In real life Mrs. Waverly had one of those faces you could read like a book. One glance and you could tell if she was angry (which she was most of the time) or pleased or impatient or whatever. But here her face was a total blank. I wondered where she was. I knew she wasn't in there (in her body, I mean), but where was she? Above us watching? In heaven? Or just gone?

Right before we stood up to leave, I got this sudden urge. I wanted to touch her to see what she felt like. I knew that was weird even at the time, but that didn't stop me from wanting to do it. In fact, if we'd been alone in the room, I think I might have. I took one last look. Real hard. And I kind of wished her good luck wherever she was.

When we got home, I sat in the car a second before getting

out. "Thanks for letting me go in there," I said. "I'm glad I did." And I wasn't sure why, but I knew it had something to do with Dad's wake.

"No problem," Chuckie said. "It was your choice." He looked at me. "Wait a minute here. I gotta check something." He reached over and felt the top of my head.

"What'd you do that for?"

"Your mother gave me a lecture about not letting you come home with wet hair. I thought I might have to hold your head in front of the heater vent."

I smiled. It didn't matter how much stuff I had going on in my life. My mom would always worry about things like whether I was risking a cold by coming home with wet hair.

That night I thought some more about Mrs. Waverly being dead and everything. Only not for so long this time. Then I got thinking about wrestling and how if I paid attention and worked hard at it I might even get good like Chuckie and end up with his build and maybe even some of his self-confidence. Then all of a sudden I found myself thinking about Miss Williams, about her voice and how pretty she was, and how she told Mrs. Beadle I was a doll. I noticed that as soon as I started thinking about Miss Williams this strange feeling came over me. It was like my whole body was hollow or something...kind of like a hunger, maybe, only more general. And it gradually dawned on me that this wasn't any regular kind of hunger, where you could do something about it and it'd be gone for a while. In fact, since I knew that empty feeling came from wanting to be around Miss Williams, the most obvious way to fill it up would be to hang around her every second I could, but I already knew that wouldn't work. Because I knew the more I hung around with Miss Williams, the hollower I'd end up feeling—like they say about an alcoholic who takes one drink and ends up wanting the next one even more than the first. It was kind of a scary, helpless feeling, like if you were sitting on a raft and could feel yourself being sucked toward some huge waterfalls, and no matter how hard you paddled, you still knew you were going over.

And suddenly it hit me. I don't know how I could have missed it, except that it was the first time anything like this had ever happened to me, and it kind of sneaked up on me when I wasn't paying attention. I was in *love!* Like in the movies and on TV. I couldn't believe it. The first real love of my life. And it was a teacher!

✧ X ✧

"Up, up, up! Come on. I know you can do it." I felt myself being lifted off the mattress—my head and shoulders anyway. It was like a pair of arms had reached in and yanked me out of this whole parade of dreams that had been marching by for what seemed like forever. I finally got my eyes open and found myself face to face with Mom.

"My God," she said. "It's like trying to wake up a rag doll."

I tried to focus on her without much luck.

"Are you awake yet? Tyler…honey?" She shook me a little. "Earth calling Tyler. Anybody there?"

"I'm awake," I said, but I wasn't too sure. I felt like I'd been through a war or something. I must've woke up about fifty times during the night. It was like I was delirious. I'd toss and turn and drift in and out of dreams, and I couldn't even always tell when I was awake and when I was dreaming. But I knew I'd had about a million dreams. And Miss Williams was in every one of them. And every one of them made that hollow feeling in me feel a little hollower. Sometimes we'd be in our classroom and Miss Williams would be running around tucking in everybody's shirttails (all the boys, that is), but whenever she got to me, she'd flit right past and start tucking in the next kid. Almost like I wasn't even there. And all the other boys would be all happy and laughing and making nasty comments like Miss Williams was some kind of floozy or something. And she'd never even hear them. Or maybe she'd hear them but she just didn't care. I couldn't tell. Other times we'd all be at Flavin's Funeral Home, and even there everybody'd be giving Miss Williams the eye. Mrs. Waverly's sons even. Which wasn't surprising since whatever part of the funeral parlor Miss Williams was in, that whole area around her seemed brighter, and everybody else, even other pretty ladies, seemed all dingy and dull compared to her. So every guy's face in the place would be following her, only the faces would keep changing. Sometimes it'd be the Coach's face, and sometimes Chuckie's, and sometimes Mr. Bailey's, and on and on until I started seeing kids too, like Lymie and Justin. But the kid who started turning up more than anybody else was Sher. And not just his face because I could see that his shirttails were out. Sometimes Mrs. Waverly would be right there standing around with everybody else, and a few times I even saw my father there; but if I tried to get close to him or talk to him or anything, he'd be gone. And where he'd been it'd be the Coach or Mrs. Waverly or somebody, and they'd start yelling at me. Only everything was all mixed up, and the Coach might be yelling about my science homework and Mrs. Waverly might be telling me to drop and give her fifty. I'd try to get away from them and get over to where Miss Williams was, but she was always on the other side of the room and she was always surrounded by people. Guys. And no matter what I did, I couldn't get close to her. No matter what.

“Are you all right?” Mom was saying. “Your face looks a little flushed.”

“I’m all right,” I told her.

“So if I let go of you, you won’t topple down in a heap again?” She let go of me one arm at a time. I stayed sitting up.

“Not bad,” she said. “I remember when it would have taken me almost an hour to get you to sit up like that in the morning.”

“Real funny,” I said. Even on good days I’m a little grouchy when I get up, and this didn’t look like it’d end up being one of my good days.

I thought about Miss Williams all while I was taking a shower and getting dressed. Only it wasn’t like I was doing the thinking. It was like the thinking was doing me, and I didn’t have all that much to say about it. Like I was possessed or something. And I had that same heading-for-a-waterfalls kind of feeling I’d had the night before. Only today I didn’t have the strength to even try to stop myself. Plus it didn’t matter what I did anyway. I already knew there was no way I could get Miss Williams out of my head. Whenever I tried to think other thoughts, she’d just end up being mixed in with them. Like if I tried to picture myself at my first wrestling match or something, instead of thinking of all the things I’d do to beat the other kid, I’d start thinking about whether I could get Miss Williams to go to the match; and even if she did go, I’d be worried whether she was really cheering for me or just sitting there thinking that wrestling was some kind of stupid, barbaric sport and I must be some kind of lowlife for doing it.

So I had to accept the fact that Miss Williams had pitched a tent in my brain, and there was no way I could get her out of there. And the strange thing was, even though I was kind of in agony, I don’t think I would have kicked her out even if I could have. Like if I had my own private genie or something, and he told me he could erase all memory of her, no sweat, I'd've told him "No thanks." Because part of me really wanted her there. It was crazy. Like deliberately sticking your hand on a hot stove or something.

Second, I knew I'd end up going out of my way to spend every minute I could with Miss Williams. Which was crazy too because I knew hanging around her would only make me more miserable and that no matter how much she got to like me, even in my wildest dreams I knew we wouldn't be dating or anything. After all, she'd already been to college and I was this eighth grader whose voice hadn't even really started changing yet. I may have been confused, but I wasn't a complete moron. But then part of me started thinking the whole idea of me and Miss Williams might not be totally out of the picture either. Not if I was patient enough. I mean, I was thirteen and she was probably around twenty-two or something, twenty-one if I was lucky. Which meant that when I got to be twenty, she'd still be in *her* twenties, and it wouldn't be all that weird for us to be seen together. At least not so weird we'd end up on Oprah or Phil Donahue or something. Plus I'm not really that bad looking. Not that I'd ever go around saying that out loud or anything, but sometimes women do consider me kind of cute. And not just my mother and people like that. Other women too. Lots of times I'd heard women telling my mother how handsome I was getting. Miss Williams herself even had told Mrs. Beadle I was a doll. And if I was lucky, as I got older I'd end up looking more and more like my brother. He was around Miss Williams's age and women were always after him. So I spent a while trying to convince myself that someday it might be Miss Williams who'd want to follow *me* around all the time. I couldn't quite make myself believe it, but at least it gave me something to hope for.

So for the next seven years I'd just have to hang on and try not to do anything stupid which would ruin my chances with her.

Seven years? I groaned. That was more than half my life.

I was still pretty out of it when I got to school. In English class we started reading *Romeo and Juliet* out loud, and I didn't even laugh when Josh Weatherby had to say "My naked weapon is out," even though all the other kids were practically rolling in the aisles. My mind knew how funny the line was, but the rest of me just sat there.

During math class, Mrs. Neibel had something hanging out of her nose and she didn't know it. And every time she'd turn around to write on the board or something, all the kids would poke each other and laugh. Mrs. Neibel knew something was going on, but she didn't know what, so she started walking around the room and stopping at different kids' desks and leaning down to give them the eye. Which only made things worse, because when she'd lean down like that, all anybody could see was that thing hanging out of her nose. So everybody ended up cracking up even harder. Except me. I still just sat there, same as I did in English.

I still wasn't myself at lunch. Travis Keegan plunked ten bucks down on the table and told Brian Maloney it'd be his if he could swallow his hamburger whole without chewing it. Brian was always making money by sucking down cans of soda in one gulp and that kind of thing. He looked the hamburger over for a minute, then took a deep breath and wrapped his mouth around the entire thing, roll and all, and pulled his lips together till it was out of sight. Everybody at our table started hooting and cheering and drum rolling as Brian's eyes started bulging out. You could see him trying to work the burger back toward his throat. Travis started yelling that he was cheating because his jaw was moving a little bit, and Travis was afraid he was working on it with his teeth. A minute later Brian started gagging and spit the whole thing out on the table. And even though his money was safe by then, Travis kept pointing at the thing and yelling, "See! What'd I tell ya? Teeth marks!"

And I didn't even laugh or hoot or anything. I was so depressed, the whole thing just seemed stupid. I had hoped that after a while I'd settle into the day's routine and kind of get back to normal a little bit. But it was like all my emotions (the decent ones anyway) were being held hostage by Miss Williams. Between every single class I'd find myself sneaking past her room just to get this little glimpse of her like I was some kind of Peeping Tom or something. And if I saw her, I'd take off like a shot because I'd be afraid she'd look out and see me looking at her. Most of the rest of my time I spent wishing I was in science class because then I'd have forty-five minutes of pure uninterrupted staring at Miss Williams, and she wouldn't know the difference because kids are supposed to look at their teacher while she's teaching. Only before I'd have a chance to get excited over that thought, I'd get depressed worse than ever thinking about how I'd have to pack up and leave when the bell rang and not see her again for a whole day unless I slunk back to sneak some more peeks, which I couldn't keep doing forever. My whole life was going crazy!

I made it to science before anybody else, which was becoming pretty routine for me. Miss Williams was sitting at her desk looking over some papers. There was nothing on the board to erase, and I didn't see anything that needed to be put away or straightened up or anything, so I went back to my seat and pretended to be looking at my science book. Actually I was peeking over it at Miss Williams. I know how stupid it sounds, but

I was kind of hoping I'd notice something about her that would disgust me, or at least prove to me that she was just another human being like anybody else. Like maybe she had a big pimple that I hadn't noticed before that was all set to pop, or her teeth were coated in green slime or something—anything that would start to free me from the hold she had on me so I could go back to living my regular life again.

No such luck. In fact, if it's possible, she looked better than I remembered her. Just to see how smooth and ivory-white her skin looked against her silky auburn hair was enough to give me this hollow ache in my chest. Plus she had on this delicate-looking pink blouse with little ruffles around the neck, and it billowed out all down her long, slender arms and narrowed around her wrists. If anybody else had been wearing that blouse, it would have been just a nice blouse. But on Miss Williams it became...I don't know...almost sacred or something. And even though I figured it was probably kind of sick, I knew that I would have given almost anything to be able to have that blouse—just to have it hanging up where I could see it whenever I wanted, or maybe feel how soft it was.

"Tyler?" I heard from way off. It was this gentle voice like my mother uses when she's trying to wake me up and she's not mad yet. "Tyler?"

I focused in. Miss Williams had been talking to me. Oh, God! I was staring at her blouse like some kind of pervert, and she was looking right at me!

"Huh?" I said and tried to look her right in the eye. I felt like a mouse looking up at some eagle who's about to swoop down on it. Only this eagle was smiling the sweetest smile you could ever imagine. And with perfect teeth.

"You're a real dreamer," she said. "It wouldn't surprise me if someday you become a poet or a philosopher."

I didn't know what to say, so I just sat there and maybe gave a little shrug. Miss Williams kept smiling.

"I was saying I heard you were on the wrestling team."

"Yeah," I said, sort of surprised.

"That's wonderful," she said. "And what an honor for an eighth grader to make a high school team! You must be very proud."

"They needed kids," I told her and right away wished I hadn't. At least I hadn't said they needed *little* kids.

That was all we said to each other. By then all the other kids were filing in, and some of them had questions about homework and stuff that she had to answer. Which was just as well because I knew I wouldn't've been able to handle some big conversation when practically the only thing I could ever think of to say to her was "huh" and "yeah."

When class started, I was able to sit back and think about things. At first I'd cringe when I thought about how Miss Williams had caught me staring at her blouse, and how when she talked to me I couldn't even answer like a normal person. But then all of a sudden it hit me. She *liked* me. She must've really liked me. I looked at all the facts. First off, right from Day One she'd told me that she'd never forget my blue eyes, and that same day she'd said how we'd both have to look out for each other since we were both new. Then yesterday she'd told Mrs. Beadle I was a doll. And finally—I couldn't believe it—she'd been checking up on my private life. She knew that I was on the wrestling team, and we hadn't even had our first meet yet. Plus she showed that she didn't just think I was some dumb jock who couldn't talk by saying she bet I'd end up being a writer or a philosopher or something. I couldn't believe it. If I played my cards right, I might not even have to wait seven years.

I sat there and watched her for the rest of the period. And whenever she happened to look my way, I'd wonder if she did it on purpose. I wondered if it was possible that she was thinking about me as much as I was thinking about her. And I started thinking that…yeah, maybe she was!

✧ XI ✧

By the time I got to practice I was really psyched. I figured maybe someday I could get Miss Williams to show up for one of my matches, and I wanted to make sure I won. Or at least that I didn't get slaughtered and end up looking pathetic. So right off the bat I went all out. When we ran the stairs, I passed everybody and finished first. And I went through the ten-point drill like I was trying out for the lead in a Rambo movie or something. If I lost my first match, it wouldn't be for lack of trying.

After that, we sat around the mat for a few minutes while Chuckie gave us this pep talk. He told us that starting tomorrow some new kids might be joining up, and if they did, we'd all have to work for our position on the team. The best kid in each weight class would wrestle varsity, and the second best kid would wrestle junior varsity. Nobody seemed too surprised about the announcement. When word spread that the Coach was out for the season and Chuckie was taking over, more kids got interested right away. And when word got around how

Chuckie was going to teach us that whole acrobatic routine he'd done for us, some of the basketball players even started wishing they'd gone out for wrestling. At least that's what Lymie heard.

When we paired off for takedown drills, I ended up with Lymie for a partner. And after listening to Chuckie's pep talk, I was more psyched than ever. I was bouncing off the balls of my feet, and Lymie was standing there shaking his head when I heard the whistle. Before he'd even rocked off his heels, I sneaked under him like a shot and drove for his legs for all I was worth, dumping him on his back in about two seconds flat. Lymie was so surprised about what happened that the next time the whistle went off, he lunged into me too much, and I was able to twist around and send him flying over my hip. This time his back actually slammed the mat. But that was the last time I caught him off guard like that. When he popped back to his feet, he was breathing hard and wearing this Charles Manson look. I didn't get him down again, but he didn't get me either.

I spotted Chuckie looking at me once. It was after we had switched partners, and I could still feel his eyes on me when he was blowing the whistle for us to start again. I faked a dive into Justin, and when he lurched back I took his legs out from under him. When I looked up, Chuckie was still there, rubbing his chin now, looking but not saying a word.

"What?" I said.

"I didn't say anything," he told me and walked over to check on some other kids.

He was right. He hadn't said anything. Which was practically the same as saying something, only I didn't know what it was. Even when he's not coaching, I always wonder what Chuckie's thinking.

The next time we switched partners, instead of going back

to Lymie I grabbed Roger Herrington, who was wrestling this year at 112 but who'd won at 105 in the sectionals the year before. I didn't really think I'd be able to take him down or anything, but I figured it'd be good practice trying, and then when I had to meet up with some 91-pound kids, they'd seem like a piece of cake. Roger looked down at me and smiled this smirky smile, but he crouched down into position and waited for the whistle anyway. Chuckie came back over and looked like he was going to say something, but he didn't. He blew the whistle and we started in. Roger yanked me around a little bit, but he didn't throw me or anything. I figured he was waiting for me to get off balance, so I made sure I stayed completely centered. But he stayed centered too and I couldn't find any opening at all. I couldn't get anywhere near his legs without risking giving him an opening, and I couldn't get him to lean into me no matter what I did.

"Don't play with him, Roger," I heard Chuckie say. "If you can take him down, do it."

Suddenly the world turned upside down. One second I was looking at Roger's knees, and the next second I was looking at the ceiling with this iron band clamped around my neck and this bulldozer bearing down on my chest. No air was left in my lungs, and I couldn't get any in. Somehow I managed to rap on Roger's back, and he let go of my neck and got off me. I still couldn't breathe. I rolled to my side and curled up in a little ball gasping for air.

I felt somebody's hands roll me over and sit me up. My eyes were watering something fierce, and when I opened them I could see a blurred Chuckie crouched down in front of me.

"You're all right," he said. "You just had a little wind knocked out." He patted my shoulder. "Relax, Ace. You need to get a little air back in there, that's all. Just take your time."

I closed my eyes and tried to calm down until some air started coming back into my lungs. When I opened my eyes again, most of the wrestling team was gawking down at me. As soon as Chuckie saw that I was breathing, he stood up. Roger reached down, gave me his arm, and pulled me up.

"You all right, Ty?" he said. "I didn't mean to come down on you that hard. You're so light, you just flew."

"He's all right," Chuckie told him. "You can't hurt this kid. He's like cement—not much to look at, but you couldn't hurt him if you tried." He patted me on the back. "Break's over guys. Get back to your partners."

I took half a step toward Roger before I felt a hand clamp down on my arm. When I turned around, I saw that it was attached to Chuckie.

"You're doing great," he said. "You're working hard and you're improving. But don't get cocky. You're not ready to take on the world yet." Then he turned me around and pointed me toward where Lymie and Justin were. "Partner up over there."

I didn't argue. I went over and hooked up with Lymie again.

On the way home, Chuckie told me if I got hurt I wouldn't be doing myself or the team any good. "You're an eighth grader, Ace. You're young. Don't think you have to do it all now. You've got your whole life in front of you."

"Are you mad because I slowed the practice down?"

"Do I look mad?" he said. "Do I sound mad? I'm just telling you not to go overboard." He looked at me. "Do you know how mad your mother would be if I delivered a mangled-up kid to her?"

"She wouldn't blame you," I said. "She'd just start yelling at me. It's a reflex."

He started to give me a "quit feeling sorry for yourself" look, but we both started laughing before he could finish it. I knew better than to try to get mileage out of whining in front of Chuckie. He knew me too well.

When we got home, I asked Chuckie if he wanted to work on wrestling. (Which meant did he want to show me extra stuff.)

"Sorry," he told me, "I've got something on tonight."

"Yeah?" I said. "Like what?"

He came around and met me at the front of the car. "What are you, my keeper?" He tried to get me in a headlock, but I pushed away from him.

"Oh, it's a lady, huh? The Chuckster's moving in on another lady?" I rapped his arm.

He looked at me and cocked an eyebrow. "The Chuckster just stands still and lets the ladies move in on him."

"Get out," I told him. But inside I was thinking how he did have a way with women. He really did. "Hey, Chuckie?" I said as he was turning to go to his cottage.

He stopped. "Yeah, Ace?"

"Have you ever...I don't know...liked an older woman?"

"Is this gonna be another game of twenty questions?"

"Why do you have to get like that?" I said. "I just asked one question. Have you ever liked...or maybe gone out with an older woman or something like that?"

"Get outta here," he said. "You've never asked one question in your whole life. Look, even the question you're asking now is already growing. First it's did I ever like an older woman, and then it's did I ever like or go out with one. And it's not even just a woman anymore. It's a woman or something like that." He cocked his eyebrow and looked at me.

"Well, did you?" I said.

Chuckie let out this big sigh and walked back to where I was.

"First of all," he said, "what do you mean by older woman? Are you talking about somebody your age falling in love with a high school girl—that kind of thing? Because, sure, that happened to me. It happens to kids all the time. Is that what you're talking about?"

"Maybe," I told him.

"Maybe?" Chuckie said, "Maybe!" He leaned on the hood of his car and looked at me. "Why do you always have to beat around the bush, Ace? Why don't you just tell me what your problem is, and we can discuss it like normal people?"

"I don't have a problem," I said. "I just asked a simple question. I was wondering, that's all. You don't have to get all crazy."

"I'm not all the way crazy yet, but I know you're working on that. And the answer to your simple question is yes. I *have* liked older women."

"Fine," I said and looked him right in the eye.

"Will that be all?"

"Yeah, that's all," I said and started walking toward my house.

"Fine," he said and started walking toward his.

When we got to our doors, we both kind of turned and looked at each other for a second.

"See ya," I yelled across the yard.

"See ya," Chuckie yelled back.

✧ XII ✧

THE REST OF that week and into the next week was pretty good. I still had it pretty bad for Miss Williams, so I wasn't completely back to myself, but at least things didn't seem quite so hopeless anymore. For one thing, I was getting to the point where I could actually talk to her using real conversation instead of the "yeahs" and "huhs" I used to use. Like I told her how my brother's first major film would be coming out during Christmas vacation, and how I'd watched quite a bit of it being filmed last spring in Los Angeles. And I told her I had the script in case she wanted to read it beforehand. (I was hoping I'd get her interested in going to see the movie, and then maybe, just maybe, she'd want me along so I could fill her in on background stuff.) And I told her about wrestling practice and how I'd have to work pretty hard to wrestle varsity because two more kids joined the team in my weight class. And all the while I'd be erasing her board or helping her put away rocks or doing whatever else needed doing that day.

I still dreamed about Miss Williams every night, only that

was better too. There'd still be tons of people around giving her the eye and everything, but when she'd see me, she'd seem glad, and I'd at least get to talk to her for a minute before she went back into the crowd. And I had the feeling, even while I was in the middle of dreaming, that things would get better still. So I didn't wake up feeling all depressed and miserable anymore.

I was even starting to be a nicer person. Like on Friday when Mom woke me up for school, I sat up and smiled at her. At least she said I did. She thought she was seeing things.

I spent all day Saturday at Lymie's farm, and I couldn't believe how patient I was getting. Even with Lymie's two little brothers following me around like a couple of hyperactive shadows, I didn't lose my cool once. After Lymie and I mixed feed for the cows and fed the calves and everything, we decided to work out on the floor of the haymow. Lymie's brothers were still right on my heels. At first they were exercising right alongside me, but they got tired of that pretty fast. One time I went down for a push-up and Larry (he's the older younger brother) ran over and sat on my shoulders, and Lonnie (he's the younger younger brother) sat on my butt. I pushed off the floor as hard as I could, but I didn't budge. Larry and Lonnie started laughing like hyenas and shouting, "How come you stopped, Tyler?" It bugged me a little but I didn't yell or anything. I figured that pushing as hard as I was would still be good exercise. Like isometrics or something. Finally Lymie saw what was going on and came over and swatted them off like a couple of flies.

"Just belt 'em, Ty. What's the matter with you today?"

The same thing happened with sit-ups. One of them climbed on my chest and one of them climbed on my feet and they stayed there till Lymie came over and swatted them off again.

"You feeling all right, Ty?" he said and kind of looked at me like I was from another planet or something.

But the thing was I *did* feel all right. And that was why I didn't feel like fighting with anybody. And I know I could have gone the whole day without fighting if Lymie hadn't wanted to watch that stupid movie on TV later that afternoon. I don't think Lymie and I have ever made it through a whole movie without one of us hitting the other one because we can never agree on what's good. If one of us loves it, the other one is bound to think it's pretty lame.

Things started out peaceful enough. We were all sitting on the couch in the living room, and Lymie told Larry and Lonnie they'd better shut up during the movie or else. And they did because they wanted to see the movie too. It was about this family that moves out of Los Angeles because traffic is getting so bad, plus their daughter has asthma or something, which isn't helped any by the smoggy L.A. air. Which made sense to me because that's one of the reasons my mother moved me out of L.A. Only this family must've made a wrong turn and landed in the Twilight Zone or something because I've never in my whole life seen a family that had so much go wrong for it. First they built this log cabin, and then they sat around and thought how great everything was going to be. But right off the bat the father gets attacked by a mountain lion and almost gets his arm ripped off. So I thought, "Fine. That could happen," and kept on watching. About then Lymie's mother came in and asked me if I wanted some hot chocolate and popcorn. She asked me first since I was company, but Larry and Lonnie started jumping around the couch saying how they wanted some, and Lymie started yelling at them to shut up. All that took a few minutes, and the next time I looked at the TV a bunch of wolves were chasing the family's two kids in a dogsled. The father comes running up and starts beating the wolves over the head with a snow shovel until the wolves finally get the message and leave, but by this time the kids and the sled have fallen through some ice into this lake. And that's only the beginning of their trouble. That night, after they get the kids thawed out, a wolverine or something sneaks up on their cabin and—I'm not sure how this works exactly—he sprays their whole supply of meat so it's all ruined, and they're worried that they won't have enough food to get by on. Pretty soon Lymie's mother along with his little sister Susan came in with the hot chocolate and popcorn, and Larry and Lonnie were so excited they started jumping around and yelling and almost spilled everything all over the place. By the time things had settled down enough so I was able to look back at the TV again, the kids were lost in the middle of this blizzard. Which about does it for the mother. She's been complaining a little all along, but now she's practically having a nervous breakdown or something, crying hysterically and saying how she wants to go back to L.A. And the father talks her out of it in about two minutes by reminding her what the freeways are like during rush hour. I couldn't believe it.

"Oh, God," I said to myself before I even realized it.

"What?" Lymie had to know. You could tell his ears had been pricked up all along waiting for me to say something.

"Nothing," I told him.

"No, you said something. I heard you. Say it again."

I looked at him. And I figured there was no way to avoid this one. "I said, 'Oh, God,'" I told him. "I mean the whole family almost gets killed fifty times in three days, and he's telling her that at least they don't have traffic problems. Gimme a break."

"It wasn't three days, lamebrain! If you were smart, you'd've noticed that when they got there it was summer, and now it's winter. Duh!"

"Yeah, Lyme. This is an intelligent movie, you gotta admit.

If they get attacked by Indians or something, what's he gonna do—remind her about the checkout lines at the supermarket?"

"Shut up," he said. "I hate watching stuff with you. You always have to analyze everything. Why can't you just watch it and shut up?"

"I tried to," I told him. "You're the one who was sitting there with your ears sticking out a mile just waiting for me to say something."

Lymie's father had come into the living room in the middle of this whole exchange, and now he was unfolding the paper and looking over the top of his reading glasses at us. He didn't look like he was ready to yell or anything. He had that same look he wore whenever he watched Lymie and me fight. Kind of philosophical and curious but not mad. When Lymie and I got done arguing, he lowered his eyes and disappeared behind his paper. Lymie went back to watching the movie and I picked up a *Farm Journal* from the coffee table and started reading this article about no-till corn. I was about three paragraphs into it when I heard these snarling and growling noises coming from the TV. I lowered the magazine just enough so I could see Lymie's face. He was looking back at me. Which I knew he would be.

"What?" he said.

"I didn't say anything." I went back behind the magazine. The snarls and growls grew louder and louder, and without even looking you could pretty much figure that one of the kids or somebody was about to be eaten by something. I lowered the magazine again. Lymie's eyes were still beading into me. Good mood or not, I couldn't resist. I lowered my voice to sound like the father. "I realize Sally got eaten by that grizzly, dear, but smell that fresh country air!"

Lymie came flying across the couch like he'd been shot out

of a cannon or something. Larry and Lonnie must have seen it coming because they'd already cleared out with their hot chocolate and popcorn. I jumped up to the arm of the couch to get out of his way, but before I landed on it, Lymie landed on me, and the next thing I knew we were both rolling around the floor. Lymie started pounding on my chest for all he was worth and yelling, "WHY DON'T YOU WRITE MOVIES IF YOU'RE SO SMART? HUH?"

By the time he'd yelled that a few times, I'd squirmed onto my stomach, and Lymie was thumping on my back hard enough so each thump sounded like a muffled bass drum or something. As I tried to crawl out from under him, I started hearing another bass drum sound. Only this one wasn't coming from *my* back.

"GET OFFA HIM, YA LUMMOX!" I heard.

Lymie stopped drumming on me, and I looked up. His mother had him by the collar and was pulling him off me. And since Lymie's mother was built kind of like Lymie only bigger, she wasn't having much trouble.

"WHAT KINDA WAY IS THAT TO TREAT COMPANY?" she yelled into his ear. "WHAT KINDA MANNERS IS THAT?"

Lymie had his arms up now, all ready to block in case she tried to belt him again.

"I OUGHTA CRACK YOU A GOOD ONE RIGHT ACROSS THE SIDE OF YOUR HEAD!" She faked a swat and then turned to me. "Did he hurt you, Tyler? Are you all right?"

"I'm all right," I told her, brushing myself off. I tried to say it kind of weak and pathetic, the same way Lymie would've said it if I were getting yelled at for hitting *him* at *my* house.

"SOME WAY TO TREAT COMPANY!" she said, turning

back to Lymie. "I OUGHTA CRACK YOU A GOOD ONE!" She gave Lymie one last dirty look and then went back into the kitchen.

From where I was on the floor, I looked up and saw that Lymie's father was still reading his paper, and Larry and Lonnie's eyes were still glued to the TV. Nobody but Lymie's mother had even stopped what they were doing while we were rolling around the floor, except maybe Lymie's father might've lowered the paper for a few seconds and given us that philosophical look. Lymie looked toward the kitchen to make sure the coast was clear, and then he reached down and gave me one final shot to the arm.

As I climbed back up onto the couch, I noticed that I still felt pretty good. Which was strange, seeing how my back had just taken a major pounding. But I did. I had this...I don't know...this feeling of security or something. It was the opposite of the feeling I had when my father died, and even Mrs. Waverly, or when I thought the Coach was having some kind of attack. I couldn't explain it. It was like if you came back here in a million years, you'd still hear Lymie's mom out there doing stuff in the kitchen, and Lymie's father'd be reading the paper even if the whole house was falling down, and Larry and Lonnie'd still be staring wide-eyed at the TV, and Lymie'd still want to kill me for not liking his stupid movie. I knew they really wouldn't be there in a million years, but that's what it felt like. And it felt good. Secure.

I even felt good enough to want to say something nice to Lymie so he could enjoy the movie without having to worry whether I was about to make some kind of wisecrack. I thought for a minute and then looked at him. "You know, Lyme," I told him, "actually I kinda like nature movies. They're kinda—"

That was as far as I got. Lymie wrapped his arms around my

head like a steel trap and squeezed till I thought my brains would come out my mouth.

"Go ahead," he said. "Say it! Whatever stupid thing you were gonna say—say it!" He cranked on some more pressure.

"Aaaah!" I yelled. "Let go, you idiot!"

"Aaaah! My ear!"

That last yell was Lymie's. And about two seconds later he let go of my head and started to pull away from me.

"WHAT KINDA WAY IS THAT TO TREAT COMPANY?" I could hear Mrs. Lawrence yelling. Then I could hear her belting Lymie. Rubbing my head, I looked over at them. She still had him by the ear, and with her other arm she was roundhousing him while he was busy covering his head. I had to smile. At that moment the world felt more safe and secure than it had in a long time.

✧ XIII ✧

BY THE END of the next week I could feel myself getting stronger every day. I wasn't turning into Arnold Schwarzenegger or anything, but I never really expected to. My arms were starting to get more wiry though, and my stomach was getting harder, and I felt lighter and springier both on and off my feet. Every morning I'd spend a few minutes in front of the mirror studying my chest and shoulders and everything to see how I was doing. I had a long way to go for sure, but at least I felt like I was on the way.

Of the new kids in my weight class, it was starting to look like only Scott Malecki would give me a real run for my money. The other kid, Arnie Tucker, was a decent wrestler, but he wasn't much on learning new things. Whenever Chuckie showed him a new takedown or escape or something, he'd try it a couple of times, and when it didn't work right off the bat, he'd go back to doing it his old way, which was just muscling his opponent into the mat. Which worked for the first few days since Arnie was stronger than either Scott or me. But every time Chuckie'd see any of us get taken down or about to get pinned, he'd come over and show us what it was that we'd done wrong. And since Scott and I hung on every word he said, and practiced every single move he showed us until we got it, pretty soon Arnie had trouble yanking us into precarious positions. And not only that, but by throwing his strength around without paying any attention to technique, it got easier and easier to catch him off balance.

So my shot at wrestling varsity seemed to be about fifty-fifty.

Things were going pretty decent in the Miss Williams department too. Whenever I stayed after class to help her with something (which was every day), she'd ask me how things were going with wrestling and everything, and it was getting easier for me to think of things to say without being in a panic all the time that I'd say something stupid. She really seemed interested in everything I said.

Mary Grace was the first to notice how much I was hanging around Miss Williams. Since we'd been in the habit of walking to our lockers together after science class, it probably seemed strange to her that I'd always find some excuse to lag behind. At first she'd ask me if I was coming, or if I wanted her to wait, but after a few days of that she just started leaving without me. Which made me feel guilty. I knew I should explain to her what was going on, but I didn't know what to say. I wasn't even sure I knew what was going on myself.

Thursday afternoon Mary Grace was waiting for me by my locker. And she *was* waiting for me. She didn't even pretend to be looking for a book or anything. In fact, her locker was closed and she was leaning up against it, watching me come down the hall. She kept watching while I plunked my books down and started working on my lock.

"What?" I said finally, when I realized she wasn't going to

stop looking at me. "What'd I do?"

She studied me a while longer before she said anything. "You're gonna get hurt, you know."

I stopped what I was doing. It kind of took me by surprise, her being that blunt. "Whaddaya talking about?" I said and went back to trying to sort out the books I'd need that night.

Mary Grace didn't answer. And what was strange was that she didn't even help me pull out the right books, which she usually did because she knew better than anybody that on my own I never ended up with everything I needed. She just folded her arms and kept looking at me.

I don't always quite know how to deal with Mary Grace. If it'd been Lymie or one of the guys, or even a girl like Babette Flosdorf, they would've told me how stupid I was for hanging around a teacher, and I would've told them to shut up and mind their own business, and we might've started hitting each other (Lymie and me anyway), or we might've just yelled at each other for a few minutes and that'd be that. But with Mary Grace...I didn't know how to respond.

"I don't know what you're talking about," I told her after a while. I said it kind of feebly, and I still couldn't look her in the eye.

"I know you, Tyler," she said. "And I know how sensitive you are." She put her hand on the top of my head and twisted it till we were eye to eye, the same as my mother would have. "Keep this up and you know you'll end up with your feelings hurt."

I pulled my head away. "I can take care of myself, *Mom.*" I slammed the locker door and started for the gym.

"Yeah, right," was the last thing I heard her say.

That afternoon the odds of me wrestling varsity increased all of a sudden. Only not the way I wanted them to.

We'd finished running the stairs, doing our ten-point drill, and practicing takedowns, and we were just starting in on some mat work. My partner at the time was Lymie, and we were working on a couple of new escapes from referee's position that Chuckie had shown us. I had my hands full with Lymie. I think after that day last week when I took him down twice in a row, he'd made some kind of a solemn pledge to himself that nothing like that would ever, *ever* happen again. It didn't matter if he was in defensive or offensive position, his whole body'd be tense and ready to go. There was no more off-guard to Lymie that I could find.

So I wasn't much aware of Scott and Arnie wrestling off to our side. And I didn't see it happen or hear the snap or anything, although for the next few days I kept hearing that sound (or at least the way I thought it would sound) and seeing it happen over and over again in my mind. Actually, I didn't see Scott until he'd already stood up. He took a couple of staggering steps and then just stood there looking over to where Chuckie was. He was wearing kind of a dumb, pathetic look, and the first thing I thought of was how he looked like Oliver Twist in that scene where Oliver wanted more soup. The next thing I noticed was his arm, which was swinging back and forth from where there wasn't supposed to be a joint.

Chuckie was there before the rest of us even got done blinking. He slipped around behind Scott and steadied him with a one-armed bear hug. Then he told Ox to go into the coaches' office for the first aid kit. By then I'd woke up enough to grab a folding chair off the side of the mat and bring it over to where they were, and Lymie and I helped Chuckie lower Scott onto it. Scott's whole body was trembling, but so slightly you wouldn't even know it if you weren't touching him.

"That kid's green," I heard somebody behind me saying.

Which he was, kind of, although not like any green I'd ever really seen, except maybe for that kind of tarnish that grows on copper pennies sometimes. While Chuckie wrapped Scott's broken arm in this inflatable plastic thing he'd pulled out of the first aid kit, I held onto his good arm because I had the feeling he might pass out any minute. Even though I'd never broken a bone, I had a pretty good idea what he was going through. He winced a few times as Chuckie straightened his arm out and started to inflate the thing, but other than that he was completely quiet. A couple of times tears rolled out of his eyes, but he never said a word. I wasn't sure if he was being brave or if the whole experience hadn't sunk in yet. I do know it took a few minutes just to get his locker combination out of him so we could get his clothes, and if I hadn't known which locker was his, we never would've found it because he couldn't remember what number it was.

When I was grabbing Scott's clothes, I noticed he had one of those hooded pullover sweatshirts which I knew would be really painful for him to get into, so I went to my locker and got him my aviator's jacket, which was zippered. And while some of the guys were helping him get dressed for the trip to the doctor's, I offered to go to his hall locker and get any school books he might need.

Lymie poked me. "You don't break your arm and then go home and do math," he told me, rolling his eyes.

I guess I might've been overdoing it. It was just that I was already starting to feel guilty about the whole situation. I didn't have anything to do with Scott breaking his arm, but I knew I'd be the one cashing in on it. Even while I'd been opening his locker, part of me was already thinking how now I'd be able to invite Miss Williams to our first meet because it'd probably be *me* wrestling in it. Which didn't mean I didn't feel bad about

Scott being in pain and not being able to wrestle and everything. I really did. Scott was a good guy, and we'd practiced together enough that week so we were well on our way to becoming pretty decent friends. But beneath all that was this part of my mind that didn't think about friendship and loyalty and all those things. It only had its eyes on ways to be around Miss Williams more, and I don't think it cared if everybody in the school broke his arm if that's what it'd take. Which made me feel a little like the girl in that movie *The Bad Seed* who ran around drowning people and burning people if they happened to get between her and what she wanted. And I don't think she could help doing what she did any more than I could help thinking what I did.

Chuckie told Ox and Victor to lead us through calisthenics, and he left to take Scott to the doctor's, where Scott's father would meet them. Later, as I was walking home I tried not to think about Miss Williams because thinking about her made me feel good, which then made me feel bad because it'd remind me what a lowlife I was. I knew I should feel bad enough about Scott's arm so I wouldn't even be able to think about how good it would feel showing off and wrestling varsity in front of Miss Williams.

About halfway home I happened to stick my hands into the pockets of Scott's sweatshirt, which I was wearing. I felt this little piece of paper in there and pulled it out. It was a page ripped out of an assignment pad, and it felt soft and smooth like paper gets after it's been in your pocket for a while. I knew I shouldn't have read it, but I figured what could be that personal about something written on an assignment pad and stuck in a sweatshirt pocket. So I opened it. The penciled-in letters had already started to fade enough so I had to stop under a streetlight to read them. Written across the top I saw "GOALS FOR

FRESHMAN YEAR." And under that, a list:

1. Get an overall B average with at least a C in math
2. Bench press a hundred pounds
3. Read a book
4. Be nicer to Julie

I smiled. It's kind of funny the different goals people have, and it's even funnier to see them written down. I wondered who Julie was. Probably a little sister or something. And I wondered if he'd made a B average so far, or if he'd managed to read a book yet. It's funny. I liked Scott more than ever just because I'd read his little list of goals. I could just picture him getting the list out and reading it every morning on the way to school. And even though I get decent grades without really trying, and even though I don't have a sister, and I read books, and I didn't really think I'd be benching any hundred pounds too soon, I was starting to feel that Scott was just like me. His mind was probably spending a lot of time mapping out its plans and hopes and goals, same as mine was.

As I went to stuff the list back into the pocket where I'd found it, I noticed something else on the bottom of it—a little arrow pointing to the side, which meant "over."

I stopped walking again and flipped it over. What I saw made me gulp. Written in ink and in all capital letters was his last goal, which he must have just added:

5. MAKE VARSITY WRESTLING TEAM

And under that were these four three-dimensional exclamation points.

I didn't do it, but all of a sudden I felt like I wanted to cry.

✧ XIV ✧

On Friday, even though I still felt bad about Scott missing out on goal number 5, and even though I felt guilty about ditching Mary Grace again, I still stayed behind after earth science class. And I didn't have to look too hard to find something to do either. All Miss Williams's general science classes were doing osmosis experiments and were proving that eggs have this semi-impervious membrane under their shell that lets some things through and keeps other things out. So with that many eighth graders handling raw eggs all day, you could figure there'd be something to clean up, which there was. On the floor over by the window where the egg cartons were stacked were the remains of at least one egg, and one of the cartons itself was leaking all over the window ledge. I grabbed a handful of paper towels, wet them down, and started cleaning the egg off the floor. I was almost done with that mess when I felt this hand on my shoulder. I almost had a heart attack. I knew who it was. There were only two of us in the room.

"What did I ever do to deserve you?" I heard Miss Williams say. "You *are* precious."

"Thanks," I said because I couldn't think of anything else. And then without looking up, "Somebody dropped an egg here."

She gave my shoulder this little squeeze and went back to cleaning up other messes and putting things away. I finished mopping up where the egg had leaked out of the carton, and then I walked up behind her. I didn't know exactly what I was going to say.

"You ever been to a wrestling match?" I heard myself asking her. "The real kind," I said when she looked back at me. "Not the TV stuff. The kind we do in school. Well, you know...after school."

"No," she said. "I never have."

"I bet you'd like it. It's not that violent or anything. They have pretty strict rules. It's a regular sport and it's kinda fun to watch." I'd never been to a school wrestling match in my whole life, so I didn't know if they were fun to watch or not, but once I started rambling there was no turning back.

"I think I might just try that sometime," she said.

"There's a decent chance I might be wrestling varsity this year," I told her.

"I know," she said. "I understand you're doing very well."

"Yeah?" I answered, kind of surprised. "I don't know. And even if I do wrestle varsity, I'm not sure I'll win because most of the guys I'll have to fight...wrestle...will be older, and they'll have more experience and everything." I shrugged.

"Well, I'd love to come and cheer for you, Tyler. You let me know when, and if I can make it, I'll be there."

"Yeah?" I said, backing out toward the door. "I will. I'll let you know."

✧

That afternoon I worked out so hard I almost passed out. In fact, I might have, a little. We had run the stairs, and I came in first, three laps ahead of everybody else, so I did jumping jacks on the stage until the rest of them got there. Next we went through the ten-point drill, and then Victor and Ox started leading us through calisthenics, which we usually did only at the end, but Chuckie had started the practice by telling us that in addition to learning new techniques, we'd be working out harder because we needed to be in way better shape for our first meet. And then he said, "Remember, if you train like a madman, only a madman can beat you." Which made sense to me, so between exercises when everybody else'd take a few seconds to catch their breath, I kept going, figuring if I could turn every practice into one continuous movement, by the time I had my first match there'd be nobody in better shape than me.

Everybody had just stopped doing squat thrusts and I was kind of running in place when all of a sudden the whole room started to get darker. Next thing I knew I felt this hand clamp down on my arm, and I heard this voice coming out of the distance saying, "...a little tipsy, huh?" Which turned out to be Chuckie. Before I knew it, he had me sitting on the floor with my back against the wall, and all these faces were gawking down at me.

"You all right, Ace?" Chuckie said, studying me.

"I'm all right," I told him.

"How many fingers?" he said, and then he didn't hold up anything but his fist.

"Eleven," I said, getting up. "Don't worry. I'm all right."

Chuckie just looked at me and didn't say anything.

"Hey, Chuckie," I said. "When's our first wrestling meet?"

"I don't believe you," Chuckie said, shaking his head and

looking at me like my face had just fallen off or something. "You black out. We have to prop you up against a wall. You're still as white as a ghost, and all you can say is 'When's our first wrestling meet?' What's the deal? You got your eyes on the Olympics or something?"

"Maybe," I said. "So when is it? Do you know yet?"

He shook his head again and then shrugged. Then he thought for a second. "Wednesday. Not next Wednesday but the Wednesday after. It's non-league, but it'll give us an idea of what we've got here."

"Great," I said. "I want to be ready." I turned to go back to my section of the mat.

"Hold it!" Chuckie said.

I held it.

"You—calisthenics!" he said to all the other kids. "You—stay here!" he said to me.

Everybody spread out across the mat, and Victor started counting off sit-ups.

Chuckie looked down at me, and he wasn't smiling. "You won't be ready for any meet if you kill yourself first." He rocked my head back and looked into my eyes. "Your eyes are still practically glazed, for crying out loud. Look, I want you to take ten. Get out of here for a few minutes. Walk around. Take a few deep breaths. But no running. And no jumping jacks. Nothing. Or I'll see that you don't wrestle in that first meet or any other meet. You understand?"

I nodded.

"Listen," he said. "That madman lecture wasn't for you. You're crazy enough already." He clapped me on the back and pushed me toward the steps to the gym.

Two minutes later, I was in Miss Williams's room. Not that I'd planned on ending up there. But one minute I was walking down the hall trying to cool down enough so Chuckie'd let me keep practicing, and the next minute I was standing in front of her desk.

Miss Williams wasn't there. Which didn't surprise me, seeing how it was past four o'clock and most of the building had already cleared out. I stood there looking at everything on her desk. I know it's weird, but I could have stayed there forever just studying all her stuff. Everything on the desk had this Miss Williamsy quality to it. Like it wasn't just regular teacher stuff but something special. But not because the stuff itself was special—only because it *was* Miss Williams's stuff, and she'd touched it and been around it all day. There was a clear glass apple that one of the classes had bought her last year when she finished student teaching. And there was a fountain pen in a black plastic holder. And a bunch of textbooks in a small wooden rack. And an ink blotter in an ink blotter holder. And that was it. She kept a pretty neat desk.

After I'd pretty well studied everything from the front, I went around behind the desk and rested my hand on the back of her padded swivel chair. I stood there for a while feeling the material, which seemed to be some kind of black acrylic, and just from doing that, I swear I could almost feel a tingling sensation running up my spine. That sensation stopped when I all of a sudden happened to think how less than two weeks ago the chair I was busy feeling had belonged to Mrs. Waverly. For a few seconds I even got a creepy feeling that Mrs. Waverly's spirit might be giving me a dirty look for having my grungy paws on her chair. But then I decided not. None of the stuff—the chair, the blotter, the desk—seemed much like Mrs. Waverly's anymore. It had already taken on a kind of Miss Williams glow, a kind of holiness almost. Like I was standing next to a shrine or something. Even the plastic pen holder and the acrylic on the chair seemed holy.

I knew thinking things like that was weird enough to be scary, so I yanked the chair out and sat on it, figuring that'd remind me that it was just a piece of furniture. Only the first thing I was aware of was the feel of the acrylic on the part of my legs that wasn't covered by my gym shorts and I started to get that tingling feeling again. So I slid forward so only my butt was left on the seat and propped my elbows up on the desk. Then I checked out the view of *my* seat from there—the second seat in the third row from the door. The view was pretty good from Miss Williams's chair, only about fifteen feet away and no obstructions. I wondered what I looked like from her desk, and also if she thought about me much while she was sitting there. When I got done thinking about that, I picked up her apple and started studying it. The first thing I noticed was how it wasn't completely clear but had all these little specks in it which seemed like they might be tiny air bubbles or something. They were probably imperfections, but to me they made the apple seem all the more perfect, which I didn't really understand, but it was true. I held it up against my cheek and closed my eyes and felt how cool it was.

"Hey, don't try eating that thing!"

I must've jumped a foot in the air. Then looking over toward the doorway, I saw George, the old after-school janitor, standing there wearing this big toothless grin. When he saw the bug-eyed look on my face, the grin exploded into this huge "rah, rah, raaaahhh!" belly laugh.

"Look," he told me once he settled down, "you'll just bust your choppers on that thing. It's the red ones you're supposed to eat! Rah, rah, raaaahhh!" He started push-brooming his way toward me.

"I wasn't going to eat it," I said, plunking the apple back on the desk. "I wanted to see Miss Williams."

"You and me both! Rah, rah, raaaahhh!" He had reached the front of the room, and he and his broom were making kind of a three-point turn. "Yessir," he said, stopping and thinking, "I never mind seeing her myself."

I waited for the nasty little chuckle that most guys give after they say something like that, but it never came. George stood there for a few seconds nodding his head and looking kind of dreamy, and then he started pushing the broom toward Miss Williams's desk.

"I'm supposed to be at wrestling practice," I said, "so I better go." I scooted for the door.

"Hey, kid!" George yelled just before I got out of the room.

I stopped and looked back at him. He looked all serious.

"There's a bowl of plastic fruit up there in the home ec room if you're still hungry."

I could still hear George "rah, rah, raaaahhhing" when I was halfway down the hall. I had to even smile a little myself.

✧ XV ✧

THE FIRST THING I did on Monday was to race up to Miss Williams's room and plunk this little piece of paper down on her desk.

"What's this?" she said, looking up at me kind of surprised.

"That's when my first wrestling match is," I told her, still a little out of breath from hurrying so much. "Remember? You wanted to know."

She looked down at it and then up at me. "I'll be there," she said, smiling. "I'll put it on my calendar right now so I won't forget."

The rest of the day I had this kind of glow just from knowing I was on Miss Williams's calendar. I almost couldn't believe it. Less than two weeks away and Miss Williams would be going to see *me* wrestle.

After science class when I was helping Miss Williams put stuff away, she seemed interested in finding out more stuff about my family and everything. Like what was my mother like and would my brother be around for Thanksgiving and that kind of thing. Thanksgiving was that Thursday, and I figured that was what got her thinking about family things. I told her some stuff about my mother—like how she was always making speeches in favor of rain forests and stuff like that—and how my brother'd be in Seattle doing a few weeks of location shooting for the new picture he'd started so he wouldn't be around for Thanksgiving even though we'd thought he would be and I was kind of disappointed. Then I told her how it was good that we had Chuckie and Mrs. Saunders around because we considered them to be like family.

"That's wonderful," she said. "It's wonderful to have family around, especially on holidays."

"What about you?" I said. "Is your family around?"

"My parents live in town," she said, "but they go to Florida for the winter, and they left last week. And like you I too have a brother who lives in California. Mine's a lawyer in San Diego."

"So nobody's gonna be around for Thanksgiving?" I said.

"Not this year. Most of my parents' people live in Columbus, Ohio. That's where my parents are from originally."

I all of a sudden got an idea. It came to me so fast I didn't even have time to chicken out.

"We'll be having this big dinner," I told her, "and it's always nice to have lots of people around for Thanksgiving, like you said—and you don't have any relatives around or anything so..." I'd been going about ninety miles an hour, but suddenly my mouth ran out of steam and skidded to a stop and I just looked at her.

She smiled at me. "I know what you're trying to say, Tyler, and I think it's so sweet of you to make me feel so welcome." Then she paused and said, "Will you ask your mother if I can bring something?"

"Huh?" I couldn't believe it. It was getting like she could read my mind.

"Let me bring something. A dessert or a salad? It's the least I can do. It'll make it easier on your mother, and you've done so much for me."

"No," I said, almost passing out from being so surprised. "We've got food. Just bring yourself." By then I was backing out the door. "I think we eat at two o'clock. I'll let you know for sure. But you can come earlier if you want."

"I'm really looking forward to it, Ty."

As soon as I got out of sight I stopped and leaned up against the wall. I couldn't believe it. Miss Williams was coming to *my* house for Thanksgiving. Like a date almost. And she was looking forward to it. Then I remembered how she'd called me Ty. Not Tyler anymore but Ty. And she'd kind of breathed it. Over and over I kept hearing the way she said it. I couldn't believe it. I mean, Mom used to always tease me about how I was so cute that pretty soon I'd have all kinds of girls chasing me every which way, but I never dreamed it'd be this easy. And I bet she never figured pretty teachers would want to come over to the house to see me. I couldn't believe it even, and I heard it with my own ears.

That night I told Mom we'd be having an extra guest for Thanksgiving dinner, but I didn't tell her who. Mainly because I couldn't think of a way to slip it into the conversation that the guest was my science teacher. It wasn't that I thought she'd fly off the handle and start screaming and yelling or anything because I knew she wouldn't. She's basically one of those parents who thinks you should listen to your kids and talk things over with them, even though she's not against yelling if that doesn't work. And I knew she wouldn't laugh at me because she'd be afraid that might damage my psyche or self-image or something. About the only bad thing she might have done is given me one of her "oh, that is *so* cute" looks, which, come to think of it, has probably damaged my psyche over the years more than any laughing or yelling would have. So I thought about it for a while and decided I wouldn't say anything about who it was. I'd just let Miss Williams show up, and then I'd introduce them right on the spot. Then Mom wouldn't even be able to give me that look.

And I wouldn't be telling any of my friends about it either. Not Mary Grace because she'd be all concerned again. And not Lymie because first he'd call me a jerk and tell me I was lying, and then even after I'd convinced him it was true, he'd probably just end up calling me a jerk again.

I probably would have told Chuckie, only he never tells me anything about *his* dates. Whenever I ask him who he's bringing here or there, he always cocks one eyebrow and says something like "Well, I guess you'll just have to wait and see now, won't you, Ace?" So I figured when he tried to pry it out of me who I invited over, I'd give him the same treatment.

I brought up the subject on Tuesday when we were driving home from wrestling practice.

"Hey, Chuckie," I asked him, "did you decide who you're bringing to dinner Thursday?"

"Yup."

"Did you ask her yet?"

"Yup."

"Did she say yes?"

"Yup." Those were the kind of answers I expected from Chuckie. And I don't think he did it because he was all that secretive about his life or anything. I think he did it just to drive me crazy. It was too dark to see if he was wearing a little smirk, but I figured he was. I knew Chuckie pretty well.

"I've got somebody coming over too," I told him.

"That's good," he said.

"I've already asked her."

"Good."

"And she said yes."

"Good."

I looked at him, figuring he was still smirking, but it was hard to tell. Chuckie has such a little smirk, sometimes it's hard to see it even in daylight.

"Aren't you going to ask me who it is?" I said.

He looked at me. "Well, I guess I'll just have to wait and see now, won't I, Ace?"

I couldn't tell for sure, but I thought I heard him give a little chuckle. I reached over and punched him in the arm. I heard the chuckle again. That time I was sure.

✧ XVI ✧

I KEPT PRACTICING pretty hard all week because I couldn't get it out of my head that Miss Williams would be there to see my first match. Now it was almost for sure. Even though I was feeling pretty good about everything, I was starting to work up some serious doubts about things. My mind is funny; when things are going really bad, my mind spends all its time hoping that things will get better. But when things start looking good, like they were now, my mind starts thinking about all the things that can go wrong. It's like my mind isn't happy unless it's unhappy.

First I started worrying that I'd lose the wrestling match. I mean, I was getting better all the time—and stronger—but still, when I got to my first match I'd've only been wrestling for less than a month, and I'd be going up against a kid who'd been wrestling for three or four years maybe. What if I walked out on the mat, shook hands with the guy, and he grabbed my head, slammed me on my back, and pinned me in ten seconds or something. I could picture the guy shaking his head with disgust that he'd wasted a whole ten seconds out of his life. Then I could hear his coach saying, "What were you waiting for—Christmas?" And Chuckie'd be shaking his head over the fact that he'd put all that time and effort into coaching me for nothing. And Miss Williams would be sitting there watching the whole mess, wondering how she could've ever been crazy enough to have been interested in somebody like me. She'd feel sorry for me for being so pathetic. I didn't even want to think about it.

And I wasn't having such a great time thinking about Thanksgiving dinner either. Half the time I was afraid that something would come up and Miss Williams wouldn't be able to make it, and the other half of the time I was afraid that she'd really show up and I'd do something so stupid and humiliating that if I lived to be a million, I'd still cringe whenever I thought about it. Or that I'd be so nervous I'd do all the typical kid things like spill my milk or get snagged in the tablecloth when I got up from my chair. Or maybe I'd get all tongue-tied being there with Miss Williams in front of Chuckie and his date and Mom and Mrs. Saunders, and I'd just sit there bug-eyed through the entire meal. A couple of times I even started to hope I'd get sick. Not throwing up at the table or anything like that—which would end up being one of those things I'd still be cringing about in a million years—but coming down with something before dinner so Mom could just explain to everybody how I wasn't feeling well, and I wouldn't even have to come downstairs.

I couldn't believe it. Things were going exactly the way I'd wanted them to, and I was working myself into a state. Sometimes I wish I could become a hermit or something and live in a cabin in the woods and not have any of the worries that regular people have. Last summer on our way back from Boston,

Mom brought me to Walden Pond, the place where this guy Henry David Thoreau built a cabin so he could go off by himself and live a simple, happy life. Which I don't think did him much good. I read his book, and from what I could tell he spent practically the whole first month figuring out to the penny how much he'd spent on every board and nail in the place. And he had to tell everybody how much he saved compared to them. If he was alive today, he'd probably be running around asking everybody what they paid for their sneakers or something and then telling them he knew where they could've gotten them twenty bucks cheaper. I knew the cabin thing wouldn't work for me either. Even before I got done building the stupid thing, I'd be driving myself crazy trying to figure out a way to get Miss Williams into it. One thing I've already found out—no matter where you move to, you always drag yourself along.

To make things worse, on Tuesday we finished reading *Romeo and Juliet* in Mr. Bailey's class. I don't know why the ending bothered me so much since I'd already decided that Romeo wasn't really what you'd call normal anyway, the way he ran around threatening to stab himself every time something went wrong. Besides, I already knew that Romeo and Juliet would die at the end, so it didn't come as any big surprise to me. But when you're already developing a pretty good case of nerves, reading a play where the main characters are doomed from the start isn't exactly therapeutic.

I even got to the point where I couldn't talk to Miss Williams anymore. I'd still stay after and help her put junk away, but I couldn't think of anything to say. I'd look at her, and my mind would go totally blank. In fact, on Tuesday she even asked me if I was all right. I lied and told her I was fine.

"Are you sure you feel all right?" she asked me again. "You just don't seem to be yourself."

"I'm all right," I told her again.

"You're sure?" she said, leaning over and kind of studying my face.

"Yeah," I said. "I'm fine." I headed for the door.

"Tyler, aren't you forgetting something?"

"Huh?" I turned around and tried to think.

Miss Williams smiled. "Your books. You're leaving without any of your books."

"Oh, yeah. Thanks," I told her. I pointed to my head. "I've always been like that." I tried to smile.

"I'm so looking forward to Thanksgiving, Ty," she said.

She did it again. Ty. And nervous or not, I felt like I could melt into the floor.

"Yeah," I said. "Me too."

When I got to my locker, Mary Grace was waiting for me again. Only this time she had Babette Flosdorf with her. And before I even got my locker open, Lymie showed up. I could feel them all gawking at me as I tossed some books in and grabbed some books out along with my jacket. When I slammed the locker shut, they were still gawking at me for all they were worth.

"What's the matter with all of you?" I said. "You never saw a kid at his locker before?"

"Not one like you," Babette said.

"Yeah, well, I hope you enjoyed it," I said and started down the hall. I wasn't in the mood to listen to some big lecture, which I knew is what they were there for.

"Wait!" Lymie said, grabbing my arm. "What's this I hear about you?"

"I don't know. You tell me."

"Mary Grace tells me you're hanging around Miss Williams every day."

"So?"

"So why don't you get normal?" Babette said, sticking her face in my face.

"What do *you* know about normal?" I asked her.

"You call chasing that teacher around normal?" Babette wanted to know. "Get your head outta your butt."

"Why does everybody have to pry into my life? Don't I get any privacy? I thought this was America."

"We're just worried about you," Mary Grace said. "We don't want to see you get hurt."

"Who says I'm gonna get hurt?" I said. "Did it ever occur to you that Miss Williams might actually like me?"

"Yeah, right," Babette said.

"So you're saying she doesn't?" I was getting more annoyed by the minute.

Babette rolled her eyes. "She's not gonna fall for some skinny eighth grader. Face it, why don't ya? You're dog crap to her."

"Oh, yeah?" I said, and by now our noses were almost touching. "She doesn't like me, huh? Is that what you're saying?"

"Duh!" Lymie butted in. "Be real, Ty. Somebody like Miss Williams isn't gonna like some dufey-looking kid."

"Tyler," Mary Grace said, kind of scrunching in between Babette and me, "we're not saying Miss Williams doesn't like you..."

"Oh," I said, "so you think she might actually like skinny, dufey-looking pieces of dog crap?"

Mary Grace ignored that. "We're just saying that she doesn't like you the way you might think she likes you, the way you want her to like you."

"Yeah, well, you better tell her that," I said before I even knew it, "because I don't think she knows it. Otherwise why would she be all excited about coming over to *my* house for Thanksgiving dinner?"

You could almost hear the sound of three jaws dropping. They were gawking at me like they had been earlier, only now their eyes were a lot bigger. I knew they were trying to figure out if I was telling them the truth or if I was telling them some desperate lie just so I wouldn't look so stupid. I brushed past them and headed down the hall. Only I hadn't even gone three steps when Lymie was back in front of me.

"What?" he said.

"You heard me," I told him. I tried to push past him but he didn't budge.

"Say it again," he said. "Just to make sure I got it right."

All of a sudden Mary Grace and Babette's faces appeared on either side of Lymie's head. All three of them looked at me like I was a ghost or something. Slowly it started to dawn on me what I'd done, and I was already developing some serious second thoughts. I hadn't wanted anybody to know about Miss Williams coming over. I was nervous enough about the whole deal even when it was a secret.

"I...I invited Miss Williams to Thanksgiving dinner," I said, and I could feel my confidence deflating by the second. "Kind of...and, I don't know...she said yes." By the time I got done, I sounded kind of feeble, like I'd just gotten over a bad case of the flu. I shrugged my shoulders. "So now she's coming over."

"Wow!" That was Lymie. He was holding his head now. "Are you telling us the truth, man? Are you on the level?"

I nodded, and maybe gave a little gulp.

"Are you crazy or something?" Babette said. "You invited a teacher to dinner?"

"I don't believe it," Lymie kept saying over and over. "I must be dreaming this." He pinched me.

"Oww! Cut it out!"

"You felt that, so it can't be a dream," he said.

"Does your mother know?" Mary Grace asked.

I looked at the floor. "Not really."

"What do you mean 'Not really'?" Mary Grace said. "You either told her or you didn't."

By this time I felt like I was in one of those dreams where all your clothes disappear when you're walking down the hall or something and there's no place to hide.

"I told her I invited somebody," I said, "but I didn't tell her who."

"She's gonna have a bird!" Babette said. "She's gonna totally freak!"

"She won't," I told her and tried to sound sure. "Why should she care who I invite over?"

"Wow!" Lymie said kind of snapping out of it. "I can't believe it. Tyler and Miss Williams. Way to go, buddy!" He thumped on my shoulder.

"They'll probably fight," Babette said. "As soon as your mother sees her, it'll turn into this big rumble—"

"Yeah, right," I told her. "For one thing, my mother doesn't fight. She doesn't believe in it."

"Yeah?" Babette said. "Wait'll she gets a load of this hot number moving in on her son, and we'll see what she believes in."

"Hot number?" I said, and I could feel myself getting madder by the minute. "Why do ya gotta call her names just because she's pretty? That's so stupid!"

Babette stuck her face back in front of mine, and this time our noses did touch. "Who you callin' stupid, worm breath?"

Mary Grace pried herself between us, pushing me back with her arms and Babette with her butt. "Nobody's calling anybody stupid," she said, kind of to me since that's who she was facing. "Besides, you're arguing over nothing. It's not that unusual for a student to invite a teacher home to dinner." She turned to Babette. "His mother will probably think it's...I don't know...nice."

"Right," Babette said, "and I'm the tooth fairy. Didn't you hear him? This kid thinks they're having some kind of affair or something."

"Just shut up, why don't you, Babette!" I said. "I shouldn't've even said anything to anybody seeing how you all have this major need to *butt into my life!*" I blasted the last words over Mary Grace's shoulder and into Babette's face.

"Somebody oughta butt into your life," Babette yelled back, "because your brains are getting more scrambled every day!"

"Shut up, Babette!" I told her.

"You gonna make me?" She clenched her fists and glared at me.

I glared back at her but didn't say anything. I didn't need to add a fistfight with some girl to my list of problems.

"I thought so," she said and stomped off down the hall.

"Good riddance!" I yelled and then wung a book up against the opposite wall. It seemed to hang there for a second before it slid down to the floor. Mary Grace and Lymie watched it fall and then went back to watching me.

"I was afraid this would happen," Mary Grace said. "You're always so touchy about things."

"Oh, great," I said. "I should've known you'd say this was my fault."

"I'm not saying it was *all* your fault," she said. "But you know the way Babette is. And you know she really is worried about you."

"So talk to me, buddy," Lymie said, circling around me.

"What's the deal? You been holding out on me or what?" He came up behind me and wrapped his arm around my shoulders. "Excuse us, Mary Grace. Me and Ty got some serious guy talking to do."

Lymie started to lead me down the hall. Before we'd gone too far, Mary Grace came up and handed me the book I'd wung. She didn't say anything. I just heard her give this big sigh as we left.

All through practice Lymie couldn't think of anything else but the idea of Miss Williams coming to my house. Luckily we were kind of late getting to the locker room and most of the kids had already cleared out. And when Lymie tried to generate some excitement by telling the leftover kids about what I'd done, he didn't get two words out before Chuckie came in and told us to shut up and get a move on. When practice started, he didn't have that much of a chance to say anything, although whenever he could he'd try to partner up with me so he could pump me for details. I took him down about five times because his attention was so divided. Finally he got the idea and started concentrating on wrestling.

But it was after practice when the locker room would be totally packed that I was most worried about. Which it was when we got there. There was the varsity basketball team. (No JVs. They practiced in the middle school gym.) And there was the swimming team. And the indoor track kids. Plus the wrestling team, which had become pretty decent sized since Chuckie took over. Usually smaller kids like Lymie and me spent most of our locker room time trying to blend into the landscape because your typical locker room crowd has kind of a survival-of-the-fittest mentality. And even though Lymie and I weren't completely defenseless anymore because we had Chuckie right inside the coaches' office, we still laid pretty low most of the time. You can't be too careful around guys who dance around in their underwear singing songs where they try to find dirty words to match girls' names, and when they catch you looking at them, they stop and say, "You gotta problem?" But today I was worried because I knew Lymie was all hyper to pass on this information about Miss Williams and me. To anybody. Including, I figured, kids dancing around in their underwear.

"Don't," I said as soon as I saw his mouth getting ready to make its first move. "I'm serious. Don't say anything."

Lymie's eyes were all lit up like Christmas trees, and I wouldn't be surprised if he didn't even hear me talking to him. "Hey, guys!" he yelled, his eyes darting around the room. "Hey, guys, listen up!"

Nobody except Justin, whose locker was right next to ours, so much as batted an eyelash in our direction. Luckily. Justin stopped pulling off his wrestling shoes and looked up at him. I grabbed Lymie's arm and told him to shut up through my teeth.

Lymie, whose brain must've been affected by the idea of instant notoriety, twisted out of my grip and headed right for center stage. I stood frozen, like he was my pet cat or something running out into traffic. Lymie barreled ahead, and as he crossed in front of each row of lockers, he yelled down the aisle, "Hey, listen up! Check this out!" He even stuck his head in the shower room, cupped his hands around his mouth, and tried to shout over the sound of about two tons of running water. That last move turned out to be his big mistake because as he was backing out of the shower room, he actually backed right onto Barry Wentworth's feet, which wasn't that hard to do seeing how Barry, our basketball team's star center, had feet you could practically park a freight car on. Barry was on his way in to take a shower, and except for me seeing how he clamped his hands down on Lymie's shoulders, I'd've thought he didn't even know Lymie was there. He kept walking through the shower room door, hung a right, and in two seconds he and Lymie were out of sight. This wasn't the first time some kid with all his clothes on had been carried into the shower room, but this had to be the smoothest. The next thing I heard was this horrible roar that sounded like something that might've come from the movie *Lord of the Flies*, which was what you might call Lymie's welcoming committee, and the next thing I saw was Lymie standing in the shower room door looking like a drowned rat. His mouth was closed, finally, and as he leaned sadly against the door frame, he actually seemed to slump from the weight of his waterlogged clothes, which were busy draining into his wrestling shoes.

"I told you," I said as I arrived with his towel and shampoo. "I told you."

✧ XVII ✧

You'd think that after all Lymie's wrestling clothes probably spent half the night twirling around inside his dryer, he'd've learned his lesson, but he didn't. The next day at lunch he was back at it, trying to generate some excitement over the idea of Miss Williams coming to Thanksgiving dinner at my house. Only this time we were surrounded by kids our own age, and it worked.

"Did ya hear what Ty did?" Lymie said before he even plunked his rear end down at the table.

"Shut up, Lymie," I told him. Which turned out to be a big mistake. As soon as I said that I could feel everybody getting more interested.

"What?" Toddie Phillips wanted to know. "What'd he do?"

"Guess," Lymie told him. "You'll never guess in a million years."

"How are we supposed to know?" Jason Peters said. "Just be normal for once and tell us."

"Shut up, Lymie," I said and tried to get him to look at me

so he'd see that this wasn't one of my normal run-of-the-mill shut-ups but a real one. He started shoveling food into his face without even looking up.

"Here's a hint," Babette said from across the table. "Think of the stupidest thing he's ever done and multiply it by ten."

I gave her this fake sweet smile which I hoped said "Drop dead." She gave me the same smile back. I looked around. Everybody except for Lymie (he was busy eating) was staring at me. And even though I'd only lived in this town about six months, you could tell they were all wondering what kind of idiotic thing I'd have to do to top some of the things I'd already done.

Lymie finally looked up from his tray, all happy that everybody was so interested. "Come on," he said. "Guess."

Except for Jason groaning, nobody said anything at first. They just kept gawking at me. Which is what you'd expect. You can't just guess what somebody did right out of the blue when they might have done anything from shot a teacher to found a ten-dollar bill on the sidewalk. I was trying to decide if it'd be better for me to tell them myself or just get up and leave when Mary Grace decided to try to help me out.

"Look," she told everybody, "it's nothing to get all excited about. Really." She looked over at me. "You want me to tell them and get it over with?"

I shrugged. "Go ahead. It's no big deal." I tried to sound convincing, but I think my voice had a little squeak to it, and I had the feeling that I looked like a rabbit hiding in some thicket waiting for some wolf to reach in and drag it out.

"What Tyler did was very nice," Mary Grace started in.

"Yeah, right," Babette said and gave kind of a snort.

"It's simple," Mary Grace continued. "Tyler invited a teacher to his house for Thanksgiving dinner."

You could see all these jaws drop down.

"Schoolie!" Sher yelled, laughing and jabbing me with his fingers on the side of the head. "McAllister, you butt-lick! You brown-nosed butt-lick! You need points that bad?"

"No, no!" Lymie yelled. He stuck one hand on my shoulder and blocked Sher's head jabs with the other. "It isn't like that. This isn't any regular teacher. This *is*—"

"This *is*," Mary Grace said, cutting him off, "a teacher who doesn't have any family in the area and would probably end up home alone eating a frozen dinner in front of the TV if it weren't for Tyler."

Jason shook his head. "I don't know, McAllister. Inviting a teacher to dinner does sound like a pretty bad browning offense."

"Guys," Lymie said and held up his hands till everybody shut up. "You got this all wrong. It's not some lonely old bag. It's Miss Williams! Ty's got Miss Williams coming over to his house tomorrow!"

At some point in the last few seconds everybody's jaws must've gone back up to the rest of their faces because when they heard Miss Williams's name their jaws dropped down again.

"Miss Williams?" Toddie said, looking at me like I was a ghost or something. "At your house?"

"No!" Sher said, trying to shake this dazed look off his face. "No way, José."

"Yes way," Lymie said, thumping me on the back and then starting to knead my shoulders like I was a boxer or something. "Our own little Ty's starting to move into the big time."

"Is this true?" Jason said, leaning in a little to study my face. "No lie?"

"Yeah, it's true!" Lymie yelled. By now he was kneading my shoulders so hard I had to set my slice of pizza down so it wouldn't go flying across the table. "Ask Mary Grace how he always hangs around her room after class and starts erasing her board and putting away her rocks and everything. All this time he's been moving in on her."

"My man McAllister!" Jason said, wearing this ear-to-ear grin. "They say it's always the quiet ones you gotta watch out for. McAllister making the moves!"

Sher's face had transformed itself into the same dirty old man leer it always did when anybody mentioned women. "Putting away her rocks," he said, managing to even make that sound dirty. "I betcha never did that for Old Lady Waverly, the fat tub!"

"Hey," Babette said and cuffed him on the side of the head. "She's dead. Show a little couth, why don't ya?"

Sher's leer didn't fade a bit. "You guys remember what Miss Williams did to me last year? When I came into her room and my—"

"Don't," I said and locked eyes with him.

"Don't what?" he wanted to know.

"Don't even start to tell that stupid shirttail story. Even if it happened, which it didn't except for maybe in your dreams, nobody wants to hear it again."

Lymie and Jason and Toddie started hooting, which is what usually happens when one kid insults another kid.

Sher stopped eating and beaded his eyes into me. "You weren't even there, McAllister, so why're you acting like you know what happened and what didn't?"

"You don't even need to be in the country to know that somebody like Miss Williams doesn't spend all her time dreaming about tucking in some seventh-grade slimeball's shirttails."

"Ooouuuu!" Jason yelled with a backup of hoots and whistles from Lymie and Toddie. "He cut ya, Sher. He cut ya hard!"

"He didn't cut nothin'!" Sher said to Jason and then turned back to me. "I didn't say nothin' about her dreaming about it. I just said she tucked in my shirt, which she *did*—all the way around. And tough crap if you don't like it, 'cause that's the facts, Jack." Then he folded his arms and gave me this smug look.

"Good, Sher," I said. "You just hold on to that memory. I bet in fifty years you'll be telling that story to your grandchildren. And they won't believe it either."

By now Lymie and Jason and Toddie were clapping and whistling and hooting so much the cafeteria lady started giving them the eye. "Your serve, Sher," Jason told him.

"I ain't even gonna waste my time," Sher said to the guys. "He puts away a couple of her rocks and all of a sudden she's his property." He looked at me. "Whaddaya think, she's saving herself for *eighth*-grade slimeballs like you, McAllister?"

"Maybe," I told him.

"Yeah, well I hate to disappoint you, but *you're* the one that's dreaming if you think Miss Williams is saving herself for *anybody.*"

"Meaning?" I said, feeling the steam rising in me. I had a pretty good idea what he meant.

He didn't answer right away. He just sat there cranking on his dirty old man leer for all he was worth. Then he said real slow, "Let's just say she's been around the block a few times." He stuck his face in my face. "And I don't mean in the front seat."

I didn't even give him any warning—probably because I didn't really know I was going to do it myself. But while he was still eyeball to eyeball with me wearing that dirty old man leer, my fist whaled on the side of his head. Next thing I knew he had me in a headlock, and we were both rolling around the floor.

Mom just stared at me and kept shaking her head. Sometimes she'd look like she was about to say something, and then she'd just shake her head some more. You could tell that the last thing she expected on a school day Wednesday afternoon at one o'clock was to be sitting at the kitchen table dealing with me. Finally she let out this big sigh and started in again.

"What did he say to you?"

I shrugged. "Something I didn't like." I looked down at the floor.

"I see," she said. "Something you didn't like. And whenever anyone says anything you don't like, you hit him?"

"No," I said. "I don't always hit everybody."

I heard another big sigh come out of her. When I looked up her eyes were locked on me.

"Tyler," she said so low I could hardly hear her, "do you really think anyone was put on this planet to be hit by anyone else?"

"No," I said and shrugged. "Not just for that."

"Well, think about it," she said. "Do you honestly think that the creator in *Her* infinite wisdom…" (she put a little extra umph into the "Her" part) "looked down one day and said, 'Wait. I forgot to put people down there for Tyler to hit.' Is that what you think?"

"Her?" I said. "You really think God's a Her?" We'd already been through this lots of times and I knew she thought God would be gender-free, but I hoped maybe this'd get her off track.

"For your sake I hope not," she said, "because I'm sure a

'Her' would be getting pretty well fed up with you by now, Mister Macho Man. When are you going to learn? How many schools have to throw you out before you'll learn?"

"I didn't get thrown out," I told her. "I just got sent home for the day."

It was quiet for a minute. Then the big sigh again. "Tyler, seriously, what am I supposed to do with you—tie your hands behind your back whenever I send you out in public?"

"Then I could still kick people," I said, hoping maybe she'd see a little humor in the situation. No such luck.

"The fact is," she continued without missing a beat, "I can't control you. I can try to set a good example. I can try to reason with you. But I can't *make* you stop solving your problems by hitting. All I can do is this—" She waited till I made eye contact. "I can make you regret it every time you succumb to the urge to punch someone. And *that* I will do enthusiastically."

"So what'll you do?" I said when she paused. I knew she was talking punishment, and from the look on her face, I was afraid this time it'd be a bad one. I knew she wouldn't tell me I couldn't have any guest for Thanksgiving dinner because I'd already invited one, and that'd be punishing somebody innocent. But what she might do scared me. She might take me off the wrestling team. I held my breath while she gave me the eye.

"You will be grounded," she continued, "and I mean *grounded*, for two weeks. You will march from this house to school, and from school back to this house, and you will not stop anyplace for any reason. Not even to get a pack of gum. You may use the yard before dinner to get fresh air and exercise, but after dinner you will march to your room where you will do homework, read, or study. No TV. No music. No telephone. Do I make myself clear so far?"

So far? I gulped. I wanted to ask about wrestling, but I was afraid what the answer might be, so I just nodded and waited.

"Good," she told me. "Now as I said, this punishment will continue for two weeks. But being as familiar as I am with your temperament, it may well be that two weeks will not be enough to break a habit of a lifetime, so..." She beaded her eyes into me. "So whenever you feel you must give in to your need to strike someone, you'll be grounded again, and we'll add an extra week each time. So your next attack will cost you three weeks of freedom. And then four. And then five. And then—"

"I get the idea," I said, and this time *I* gave the big sigh.

"I wanted to make sure," she said, "so that when you end up grounded till well past the turn of the century, I'll know that you had been sufficiently warned."

"Oh, like I fight that much," I said.

"Maybe—just maybe—this will ensure that you don't." She looked me over. "Any questions?"

"Wrestling?" I kind of squeaked.

She shook her head. "I was sorely tempted," she said. "I could have used this situation as the perfect excuse to get you off that team. But since wrestling is a school activity, and Chuckie tells me you're working hard at it, I've decided you may continue. It may even be good for you in that it may allow you to burn off some of your aggressiveness in a supervised sport rather than by attacking people at random." She let that sink in. "Any other questions?"

I shook my head, even though I wanted to ask her exactly what she meant by hitting people. Like did it mean only during a real fight? Or did it mean I couldn't hit anybody no matter what? Lymie and I hit each other all the time, but it wasn't like we were really fighting or anything. So what if she happened to see me kind of routinely belting him? But I thought it was probably best not to ask that right away. With the mood she was in, she'd probably end up saying no hitting whatsoever would be allowed, and then she might ban headlocks and ear pulls and noogies—you name it. And then I really *might* end up being grounded until past the turn of the century. I figured what I'd do was just make a special effort to keep my hands off Lymie until things got back to normal.

That afternoon, while the rest of the team was at practice, I figured I should go up to my room and work out for the whole time so I wouldn't fall behind. So for two straight hours (almost anyway) I did jumping jacks and squat thrusts and push-ups and sit-ups and Chuckie's ten-point drill. I had to stop a couple of times because I got light-headed, and a couple of times Mom came in and started yelling (only she has this way of yelling without raising her voice) that I was overdoing it, so I had to spend a couple of minutes each time explaining to her that I was fine. But by the time five o'clock rolled around, my knees were like jelly and I was so light-headed I could hardly stand up in the shower. But I felt great. At least I'd know that if I lost my first wrestling match in front of Miss Williams next Wednesday, it wouldn't be because I didn't try hard enough. At least I'd know that.

✧ XVIII ✧

THE NEXT DAY was Thanksgiving. I woke up a little after seven and threw on some sweatpants and a hooded sweatshirt so I could go out and run. Which I was really looking forward to, not only so I could get into top-notch shape for wrestling, but also because a long run always has a calming effect on my nerves, and since Miss Williams was supposed to be showing up at my house for dinner, my nerves needed all the calming they could get. I must've woke up at least five times during the night, and each time I'd been in the middle of a dream starring Miss Williams. And even though in all these dreams Miss Williams was being really nice, and nothing big in the way of disasters had happened, I'd still wake up with this vague but pretty strong feeling that something was about to go wrong. That feeling hung on even after I got up.

Mom intercepted me before I even got to the front door. "And where might we be going?" she wanted to know as she stood there blocking my way with her arms folded and one eyebrow cocked up a little. Just the fact that she'd called me "we" was a bad sign.

"Running," I said. "Like I always do."

She didn't budge. If anything, she planted her feet more firmly than ever, and when I started to go around her, she stuck her hand on my chest.

"Aren't we forgetting something?" she said.

"Huh?" I thought for a minute. Then I groaned, remembering. "I'm grounded. I can't even leave the yard." I threw up my arms and turned back toward the stairs.

"Hold on," Mom said. "Come here."

I did. She stood there for a minute just looking at me.

"Listen," she said. "We'll consider this part of your wrestling practice." She grabbed me by the chin and wrapped her fingers around my cheeks. "But you don't stop anyplace for any reason. And—" She squeezed my cheeks and brought her head in closer. "And this in no way invalidates your punishment, nor does it signify any softening of my position on that matter. Do we understand each other?"

I tried to nod, but she still had a pretty good grip on my chin. She must've gotten the idea though, because she let go of my chin and opened the door for me.

"Do not pass go!" she yelled after me like we were playing Monopoly or something. "Do not collect two hundred dollars!"

Right, I thought. What I really needed was a get-out-of-jail-free card.

After I jogged and took a shower, I had to help with the dinner preparations. Mom always insisted that I help whenever we had any kind of big dinner. It's not that I was all that great around the kitchen because I wasn't (Mom usually ended up saying how it would've been easier for her and Mrs. Saunders to do the whole thing by themselves); but she wanted to make sure I realized that dinner didn't just miraculously appear on the table, and she also wanted to make sure I didn't get the idea that making dinner was something only women were supposed to do.

Even though I'd had my share of disasters over the years (like the fondue fire that cost Mom her best tablecloth and half an oven mitt), I'd gotten pretty good at two things. The first was making Shaker mashed potatoes, and the second was setting the table.

The mashed potato part I learned from my mother when I was a little kid. She grew up in Saratoga, which isn't that far from Albany, and right around the corner from the Albany County Airport there used to be this huge Shaker settlement. In fact that's where Mother Ann Lee, the founder of Shakerism, is buried. Anyway, Mom is the type who always has to learn about local culture and cuisine and all that, and then she has to make sure that some of it rubs off on me. Which explains why somebody like me would know how to make something like Shaker mashed potatoes. Besides, it's pretty easy to make them. First you peel the potatoes and cook them, and then you mash them by hand (no beaters) with butter and light cream and salt. And the last thing you do is fold in some diced onions—raw—and some dill weed. Simple, but they always get compliments like crazy.

The setting the table part came about because one year I was helping by stirring the gravy and accidentally splashed some of it on the floor, which I left there because I figured we might just as well wait till we were done cooking and clean the whole thing once, but before we got to that point, Mom stepped in it and ended up on the floor wearing this bowl of cranberry sauce. Which *I* found kind of funny but she didn't, so she tried to come up with a job for me which put me "less underfoot" as she put it. That's when she taught me all about the art of table setting, how to fold the linen napkins just right, and where to put the silverware and plates and wine glasses and all that. And I really am pretty good at it. I hardly ever break anything, and when I get done it looks like something right out of a magazine.

Chuckie dropped by and watched me for a minute as I was finishing up on the table, and then he followed me into the kitchen when I started peeling the potatoes.

"Ace," he said, clapping a hand on my shoulder, "you're gonna make somebody a fine little wife someday."

I could feel Mom's eyes moving our way. Then her whole body. I could also feel this smile growing on my face. In about ten seconds Mom was standing right next to where we were.

"Chuckie," she said, giving him the eye, "I hope you're not implying that being good at kitchen work is what makes someone a good wife." She tapped her toe on the floor and waited.

"Huh?" You could tell that Chuckie hadn't expected his stupid line to turn into some big philosophical discussion.

I stuck my face up to his ear. "Tell her they have to be good looking too," I whispered and poked him in the ribs.

Chuckie was smart enough to ignore that suggestion. He just stood there wearing kind of a pitiful smile and waited for Mom to finish her spiel.

"Because surely," Mom continued, "there can't be any men around these days, especially as young as you are, who harbor such archaic notions."

I stuck my face up to his ear again. "Tell her you think they should be able to clean and keep a tidy house too," I whispered.

This time Chuckie was ready. He grabbed me and yanked me out in front of him. "Ace!" he said in this big exaggerated way, "I'm disappointed in you. I thought you knew that women weren't put on this earth just to look pretty and clean houses and cook. I thought you were taught better than that." He turned back to my mother. "I'm sorry, Ms. L., but the things this son of yours has been saying...well, they're very upsetting to me—feeling how I do about women's rights. In fact, I'd better leave now. I'm afraid I might hit him." He pushed me away. "Maybe by the time I get back here with my date, I'll be cooled down. Otherwise I don't even know if I'll be able to eat with the likes of him." He gave me one last look and shook his head in disgust. On his way out the door we could hear him mumbling, "And in this day and age, I just can't believe it."

Mrs. Saunders was chuckling through the whole exchange. She was old enough so she really thought that women were better at cooking and cleaning and taking care of kids and all that, and she always got kind of a kick out of whenever Mom started in trying to reform any of us.

Mom looked at her and smiled. "Well, at least I made my point," she said.

Just then the potato I was peeling slipped out of my hand, went bouncing across the floor, and landed at Mrs. Saunders's feet.

"And I believe Tyler just made mine," Mrs. Saunders said and chuckled again.

About a half hour later the doorbell rang. "That's probably Chuckie with his guest," Mom said.

"Or it's my guest," I said and took a deep breath. "I'll get it."

As soon as I got out of the kitchen, I stopped and took a couple more deep breaths and wiped my eyes, which were watering a little from dicing onions. I even practiced a couple quiet "hello's" to make sure my voice still worked. I felt all of a sudden like I was in a dream, only I wasn't sure yet if it was a good one or a nightmare.

I popped the door open and there was Chuckie. And standing right next to him was Miss Williams. My jaw dropped down for a second, and then I realized they must have met walking up to the house.

"This is great," Chuckie said. "He's so happy to see us he's crying."

"Onions," I said, wiping my eyes again. "I'm dicing them."

"You recognize this lady?" Chuckie said.

"Yeah," I said. "That's my teacher." I looked at her. "Hi."

"Hi," she said and gave me this big smile which about melted me into the door frame.

Finally I managed to say, "Wanna come in?"

"I thought maybe we'd just stand here in the cold for a while," Chuckie said and kind of pushed me out of the way. He turned to Miss Williams. "Is he this slow in class?"

"He's wonderful in class," she said and gave me that same smile again. This time I could almost feel myself melting into the carpeting. Chuckie grabbed Miss Williams's arm and ushered her into the house. I wondered if that's what I should've done.

As soon as I snapped out of it, I leaned into Chuckie and said quietly, "Where's *your* guest, Chuckie?"

Chuckie pretended to be cocking his arm like he was about to give me a backhand. "Such a jokester," he said.

Even though every time I thought about Miss Williams being right there in my own house I'd almost pass out, I couldn't help but smirk a little thinking how Chuckie might've gotten stood up. I knew he kind of considered himself a real ladies' man.

Next thing I knew Mom was standing there with us inside

the door and everybody except for me was talking and shaking hands and all that. All I remember for sure is hearing Miss Williams saying, "He's my best student *and* my most charming one. I don't know what I'd do without him." And then Mom saying, "We like him too, but there are times..." and then she cocked her arm into backhand position like Chuckie had just done. I was afraid Miss Williams would start getting the idea that everybody that knew me well enough wanted to belt me.

Mom took Miss Williams's coat and handed it to me. "Would you hang this up, hon?" And then back to Miss Williams, "Aileen," (which was her first name) "we're so happy to have you here. Tyler really seems to enjoy your class, and I can't remember the last time that happened in science. And this guy..." She indicated Chuckie. "This guy is practically family, and any friend of his is always more than welcome..."

I was about to correct her when all of a sudden I experienced a blackout. Something had landed on my head.

"Take care of that too, Ace," I heard Chuckie say, "as long as you're going to the closet."

Then from under Chuckie's coat I heard it. It might have been a little muffled, but I heard it all right.

"I do appreciate this so much," Miss Williams said. "When Chuckie first invited me, of course I was delighted, but I was afraid I might be imposing on you. And then Tyler..." She pulled Chuckie's coat off my head. "Oh, Chuckie, really!... But Tyler made me feel so welcome, I can't tell you." She gave me the sweetest smile ever. Only this time I didn't almost melt into the carpet. I felt like I'd grabbed an electric fence.

"Silver-tongued devil," Chuckie said and punched me in the arm.

My jaw must've been hanging down to my chest. And I could almost feel all the blood draining from my face. And even though I was in shock, it all came to me at once: Why Miss Williams had thanked me for making her feel welcome even before I got the words out to finish inviting her. How she knew I was on the wrestling team. How she knew I'd probably be wrestling varsity. And why she'd *really* be going to our first wrestling meet. She'd been going out with Chuckie all that time.

"Are you all right?" Chuckie shook my arm.

"Great," I said and pulled away from him. "Just great."

Somehow my body managed to take the coats over to the hall closet and start hanging them up. I could feel my eyes watering. And this time it wasn't from raw onions. I couldn't believe how stupid I'd been! What a jerk!

"Come in and sit down," I heard Mom say. "We'll put Chuckie in charge of making drinks. Tyler's guest should be along any time and dinner is almost ready."

"She isn't coming," I said from the closet, only it came out louder than I wanted it to and sounded too angry. Without turning to face anybody, I headed back toward the kitchen.

"That's strange," I heard Mom say before the door swung closed behind me. "Nobody called, and he was just expecting her..."

I slipped up alongside Mrs. Saunders and picked up dicing the onions from where I'd left off. She was busy making gravy.

"Who was at the door, dear?" she asked without even looking over.

"Chuckie," I told her. "And his date." By concentrating I could make my voice sound almost normal.

"Oh, that's nice. And I hope *your* little friend is along soon. Everything is almost ready."

"She's not coming," I said, and as I started in on the next onion I could feel her looking at me.

"Oh, that's a shame," she said. "Something came up?"

I shrugged and turned my head away as much as I could. "Kind of."

"I bet she has that virus that's going around. Thelma next door told me her son and half her grandchildren came down with it. It's only a twenty-four hour thing, but when you get it, you know you've got something."

I didn't say anything. Mrs. Saunders always figured everything was caused by whatever disease was going around at the time, and that was all right with me. It saved me a lot of explanations.

The door to the dining room opened, and Mom pulled up on the other side of me. I could feel her studying me, and then her hand came down on my shoulder. "Am I imagining things or is something wrong here?"

"No," I said, still not looking at her.

"Look at me," she said.

I did, and she wiped a tear off my cheek.

"Onions," I said.

She felt my head, probably trying to figure out if maybe I did have some virus. I must have been about the right temperature because then she said, "Are you going to tell me what's going on?"

I shook my head. "I'm all right," I told her. But all while I drained the potatoes and threw in the butter and salt and light cream and mashed them, I could feel Mom studying me and thinking about what could've happened.

"It's a shame about his little friend," Mrs. Saunders said to her. "If you ask me, she has that twenty-four hour bug."

Dinner felt like it lasted three days. I tried to be polite, and even halfway cheerful, but I don't think I pulled it off too well. Every time I looked at the place setting where Miss Williams was supposed to have been I got the same terrible feeling. Part of it was plain, old-fashioned self-pity. Not because I'd been stood up, because I hadn't really. To be stood up means you were at least a contender. I was never even in the running. Which led to the second part of my terrible feeling. Every time I looked at Chuckie I wanted to hit him. Because all that time while I'd been dreaming about Miss Williams and me, and even when I was arguing with Babette and rolling around the cafeteria floor with Sher to defend her honor, Chuckie'd probably had his grungy paws all over her. Just thinking about it made me crazy.

I wasn't actually afraid of losing control and belting him in the middle of the meal or anything. And it wasn't because Mom would have added to my grounded time. I was too depressed to worry about that kind of thing. But some part of me knew this whole mess wasn't even Chuckie's fault. It was mine. I was the jerk with the out-of-control imagination. Chuckie probably didn't even know what was going on. Or Miss Williams either, I hoped. And I wanted it to stay that way, which it wouldn't if I attacked Chuckie while he was passing the cranberries or something. Besides, hitting Chuckie was kind of like hitting Superman. You could hit him until you were blue in the face, and you'd just end up hurting your fists.

Everybody knew something was wrong even if they didn't know exactly what, and I knew everybody else was trying to act normal, same as I was. As Chuckie was slicing the turkey he kept telling everybody not to eat too much of it because he wanted to make sure there'd be enough left for me. Which was supposed to be funny because I'm a vegetarian. No matter how hard I tried, I couldn't twist my face into a smile. Meanwhile, Mom was doing her best to keep the conversation going by telling about how I'd made the Shaker mashed potatoes, and after everybody got done making a fuss about them, she started talking about the weather and how she'd forgotten how cold upstate New York could be. Whenever somebody starts talking about the weather, you know there's at least a little strain in the air. And the way everybody else was joining in with their own weather opinions and stories, you could tell the whole crowd was pretty tense.

A couple of times I became aware that my fists were clenched and my eyes were beading into Chuckie. But most of the time I was just staring into my plate and trying to keep my eyes from watering. As soon as we were done with the main meal I asked if I could be excused. Mom looked me over pretty good and then kind of shrugged and said all right.

At the top of the stairs I hung back, listening for a minute, before heading for my room. I heard Mrs. Saunders say, "I think he feels bad that his little friend couldn't make it. He was looking forward to this dinner so much."

"Hmmm," Mom said, "but the phone didn't even ring."

"Well, I hope he's not coming down with something," Mrs. Saunders said. "I don't know about that wrestling business, Chuckie. He wears himself out..."

I turned toward my room. I was too depressed to even eavesdrop anymore.

✧ XIX ✧

We had practice the next morning at ten. It was supposedly optional, but it was pretty much understood that if we weren't out of town visiting family or something we'd be there. I was looking forward to it. Even though I didn't really want to see Chuckie, I did want to get out of the house. So far, I'd managed not to answer any of Mom's questions, and as far as I could tell she didn't know what happened. I think she thought I'd been stood up by some girl at school, although she didn't quite understand how I'd found out about it. Which was all right with me. As bad as I felt, I knew I could still feel worse if everybody found out what really happened. Mrs. Saunders still thought I was coming down with some virus, so she was easier to deal with. She kept feeling my forehead and bringing me ginger ale.

I decided to leave a little early and walk to practice rather than ride to the school with Chuckie. That way I wouldn't have to face him alone, and he'd be busy watching all the other kids and wouldn't be able to zero in on me and whatever he thought my problem was. It didn't work. As soon as I stepped out the front door, there was Chuckie coming up the porch steps.

We looked at each other for a second.

"Hi, Ace," he said. "How're you doing?"

"All right," I told him.

"Your timing is perfect," he said. "I wanted to talk to you before practice."

"About what?" I said, even though I knew.

"I wanted to say I was sorry about what happened yesterday."

I looked at him. "You know?"

"Yeah, I know."

I groaned and leaned back against a porch column. "Does *she* know?"

He nodded. "She figured it out before I did. The day before, one of the kids had asked her if it was true that you had invited her to dinner. At the time she thought what the kid meant was would she really be going to dinner at your house. And then she heard that the fight you were in had something to do with her. So yesterday, she put two and two together..."

"Oh, God." I went over and sat on one of the porch chairs. "She must really wonder where they dug me up."

Chuckie sat down in a chair next to me. "No, she doesn't. She likes you. She really does."

"Yeah, right," I said. Then after a while, "Did she laugh?"

Chuckie smiled. "No. Actually she feels pretty terrible about this too."

We were quiet for a minute. Then Chuckie stood up.

"I'm sorry, Ace. I really didn't have any idea..."

"You didn't do anything wrong," I told him. "All's you did was ask somebody for a date. It's me who was living on Fantasy Island."

"Well, I'm sorry we made you feel bad anyway."

"Thanks." I got up and started walking with him to his car.

"You must really like her, huh?" Chuckie said.

I nodded. "Yeah, I really do. Still. It's totally stupid and I feel like a jerk, but I still really like her."

We got into his car.

"Would you rather I didn't see her anymore?" Chuckie said as he started the car.

"No," I said quietly. "Thanks, but that wouldn't be right. Besides, it wouldn't do any good anyway. She's not going to like me even without you going out with her. The whole thing was so stupid. Let's just try to forget it, huh?"

"Forget what?" Chuckie said and punched me in the arm.

I no sooner got my gym locker opened than Lymie showed up, all bug-eyed and wearing this big grin.

"So?" he said and poked me in the ribs. "So?"

"So what?" I said, pulling my gym clothes out.

"So how'd the date go? You know, with Miss Williams?"

I shot a glance around the locker room. Everybody was busy putting on their wrestling stuff and having their own conversations, so no one seemed to be paying any attention to us. Luckily.

"I never said it was a date," I said. "I told you she was coming over for dinner. Big deal."

Justin pulled up next to us and started opening his locker. "Who came to dinner?" he wanted to know.

I groaned and sat on the bench. I knew all Lymie needed was an audience and off he'd go.

"Didn't you hear?" Lymie said to him, all amazed. "Ty invited our new eighth-grade science teacher to his house for Thanksgiving dinner. You've seen her, haven't you?" He kind of outlined her shape with his hands around his own chest and hips. "And she said yes!"

"No kidding?" Justin said. "You really did that?" He poked me in the arm. "You little tah-ger."

"So she showed up?" Lymie said, turning back to me. "She really showed up?"

"Yes, she showed up," we heard from behind us. It was Chuckie. "She really showed up. And so did I. And so did his mother and Mrs. Saunders. We all showed up. And we all ate dinner. You guys need to see a seating chart of the whole thing? But meanwhile I'm out there waiting for my wrestlers to get out on that mat and start losing some of the weight they probably put on yesterday. SO CUT THE CHATTER, GET YOUR BUTTS IN GEAR, AND GET OUT THERE! YA HEAR ME?"

I couldn't believe it. He sounded just like the old coach. He was even wearing the same kind of look on his face. We all started getting dressed like the place was on fire.

As we trotted out the door, Justin poked me again. "Tah-ger," he said.

Chuckie kept it up all during practice. Between the way he had us racing from one drill to the next and the way he just happened to come over and show us some new move every time Lymie tried to pry out of me what happened at dinner, I made it through the whole practice without having to say one word about Miss Williams. Which I was pretty grateful for. Not only did I not feel like telling Lymie what a jerk I'd been, but I also was still pretty depressed and wanted to keep busy and lose myself in the workout. Maybe it wouldn't matter to Miss Williams whether I won my first match or not, but it still did to me. More than ever. I wasn't sure why. Maybe just to regain some little measure of the self-respect I'd lost the day before. Or maybe just having a goal to struggle toward kept me from having to face head on how bad I really felt. All I know is that I worked harder at that practice than I've ever worked before, harder even than when I was trying to get into shape to impress Miss Williams. A couple of times Chuckie came over and told me to slow down a little, and finally he made me stand off to the side. When I started doing calisthenics, he ran over and started yelling at me.

"Ace, do you have some kind of hearing problem? I told you to stand over here. *Stand!* So don't do jumping jacks. Don't do push-ups. Just stand there. You aren't going to win anything next week if you burn yourself out this week. Ya hear me?"

I nodded.

"Look at you," he said. "Look at your eyes. You look like some kind of zombie, for crying out loud."

I just stood there. I couldn't very well look at my own eyes.

"What are you trying to prove working yourself into that kind of state?"

I shrugged. "I thought I'd feel better."

"Listen," Chuckie said and put his hand on my shoulder. "You're too obsessive. You have to lighten up a little. For ten minutes I want you to walk around the edge of the mat. Don't do anything but walk, and when you're done, you come over here and I'll decide if you're ready to practice anymore today." He grabbed my arm. "Look at me. If I see you doing anything besides walking around the outside of this mat for the next ten minutes, you're not wrestling at all next week. You understand me?"

I nodded. And knowing Chuckie wasn't the type to make idle threats, I started walking. Besides, I figured if I didn't get a good enough workout at practice, I could work out on my own that afternoon when I got home. Since I'd be stuck there anyway, I might as well be doing something useful.

I'd done about three walking laps around the mat when suddenly I stopped, aware that something was different about the way I felt. At first I thought maybe I was about to pass out. It felt a little like that. Almost like I was floating or something, and also like I was watching myself at the same time I was *being* myself. And I noticed that I was hardly breathing, or maybe breathing like somebody in a deep sleep. But the biggest change was that this strange sense of peace had settled around me. Strange, but also familiar. It was like being outside when it's snowing big fluffy flakes, and everything seems slowed down and calm and silent—when even a car going by hardly makes a sound. Only this wasn't quite like that because I could hear all the regular wrestling practice sounds around me as clear as ever. And I realized that the *real* silence I was feeling was inside *me*. My brain, which was usually cranking out thoughts by the barrelful, was just kind of sitting there taking everything in. And I felt this warm tingling feeling going up my spine, like when I was a little kid cuddled up in this big chair with my mother and she'd be reading me *Curious George* or something and rubbing the back of my head. It was that kind of cozy, safe feeling. And I felt myself getting this feeling from everybody around me. First I got it from Chuckie as I watched him showing Justin a new escape. Then I got it from Justin when he tried out what Chuckie had showed him. Then from Lymie, who Justin was escaping from. That tickly, tingly feeling in my spine spread all the way up and through to my head, just from watching those guys. I couldn't believe it.

"My man, John Henry!" That was Ox. He wrapped his huge arm around my shoulder. "My main man needs a partner!" He started pulling me back onto the mat.

"I can't, Ox," I told him. "I'm supposed to just walk." That tingly warm feeling now felt like it was flowing into me from Ox.

Next thing I knew, Victor Grouse was in front of us. "Come on, Ox," he said, wearing his usual Victor scowl. "Quit farting around and get your dumb butt over here."

I couldn't believe it. I even tingled from being around Victor.

"No," Ox said and towed me past Victor. "I got a new partner."

"OX!" That was Chuckie, and he was heading our way wearing his own scowl.

I laughed. The whole thing was like watching a play. Only I was in it too.

Ox let go of my arm. "Don't hit me," he said to Chuckie and gave this big exaggerated flinch, "'cause I didn't do anything wrong."

"I oughta kick you in the head," Chuckie said. "Only I'd probably break my foot. Why aren't you wrestling?" He came up and stuck his face in Ox's face.

Ox shrugged. "I had to get a new partner. Victor cheats." He pointed at Victor like a little kid.

"What are you complaining for?" Chuckie said. "*You* cheat every day."

"That's different," Ox said.

Chuckie grabbed him by the ear and led him over to the heavyweight section.

"He'll hurt me!" Ox whined. "And it'll be your fault."

"He won't hurt you," Chuckie said. "*I'll* hurt you. You're my partner now." He turned to me. "Ace, you get walking. And, Victor, you keep the time. Ox wants to go for three minutes."

"No I don't," Ox said.

"What's that, Ox?" Chuckie wanted to know, squeezing

harder on his ear. "You said you wanted to go three and a half?"

"Huh?" Ox said. "Where'd ya hear that?"

"What's that, Ox?" Chuckie said, cupping his free hand around his ear. "You wanna do four? What a great attitude. Okay, we'll do four." He let go of Ox's ear and clapped him on the back. "Listen up, everybody. Switch partners and we'll do four minutes on the whistle."

Victor blew the whistle and everybody started wrestling. I started walking again, but slower. My whole body was tingling now, even my skin, and I couldn't remember ever feeling more snug and secure. And not only that, but the whole world (meaning the stage we were on) looked brighter and better than it ever had—the blue vinyl wrestling mat with its creamy white lines, the satiny beige backstage curtain, even the brown steel folding chairs set up off to the side—they all had this dreamlike quality, while at the same time they were clearer and sharper than ever. Everything seemed so perfect. I couldn't believe this was the same world I was living in only yesterday, or five minutes ago. Even when I thought about Miss Williams I could feel a nice warm glow growing inside me instead of the sick hollow feeling I'd gotten before.

I slowed down some more, afraid if I moved too fast I'd leave that good feeling behind.

After practice I was pretty much back to normal. Lymie was still trying to pry information out of me about what happened when Miss Williams came over to dinner, and I still didn't want to tell him about it. Finally, after I convinced him that my mother didn't try to beat her up or anything and that nothing major happened, he shrugged his shoulders and shut up for a while.

I watched him for a minute as he grabbed his shoes out of his locker and tried to get a knot out of one of his laces. "Hey,

Lymie," I said finally, leaning in toward him so nobody else'd hear me, "did you ever...I don't know...did you ever have the feeling that your mind drifted off into some other dimension or something?"

"Huh?" Lymie said. "Whaddaya talking about?"

I grabbed my socks out of my locker and tried to think how to explain it. "Well, it's not really another dimension, because everything's the same. Only everything *seems* different."

Lymie's face was all scrunched up, thinking. Then he looked at me. "You feel all right, Ty?"

"I'm fine," I told him. "Just listen. You're standing there, or walking around or whatever, and all of a sudden you feel perfect—you know, tingly and happy and good all over, and you look around and everything around you looks perfect, even the people, and you just...I don't know...you just feel like every cell in your body is kinda jumping for joy."

Lymie was wearing this intense blank look, like I was talking to him in Russian or something.

I barreled forward, maybe trying to explain it for myself as much as for Lymie. "I never felt quite like that before, Lymie. I actually felt all this...I don't know...love or something, and I felt it for everybody I saw."

Lymie's face kind of scrunched up again when I said the word "love." Just then Victor Grouse strode by, naked, snapping his towel at anybody that got in his way.

"Even for Victor," I said, jerking my thumb toward Victor. "I even felt it for Victor."

Lymie turned to see Victor's bare butt disappear behind a row of lockers. Then he leaned into me and said really quietly, "Have you told anybody else about this?"

I shook my head.

"Don't," he told me.

✧ XX ✧

By MONDAY MORNING I was completely back to normal. Which wasn't good. I was back to getting a sinking feeling in my stomach whenever I thought about Miss Williams, my mind was back to racing around with about a million thoughts about things that had already gone wrong or that might be getting ready to go wrong, and (Lymie didn't need to worry) I didn't feel any love at all for Victor anymore.

My main dread was going back to school. I know from experience that when you've been through something really humiliating or suffered some kind of misfortune (not like a death in the family or anything really serious like that maybe, but most others), there's always going to be a bunch of kids waiting in the wings to give you a hard time. You always hear people who are supposed to be child experts talking about how kids are innocent and basically good until they learn how to be bad from adults. Which shows they've never really opened their eyes and looked around. I'm not saying that adults are perfect, but at least in some ways they're not as bad as kids. Like, if you see five old ladies walking down the street and one of them slips on some ice and falls, would the other four start rolling around the sidewalk cracking up and telling the old lady that fell what a jerk she is? Because that's what your average group of kids would do. And I'm even including myself. I couldn't stand around and watch one of my friends fall down without cracking up if you put a gun to my head, and most kids (boys especially) are the same way. And after the way I'd acted all smug about Miss Williams and me, and after I'd punched Sher and told off Babette, I wasn't expecting them to show me any mercy if they were to find out what really happened at my house on Thanksgiving.

Just facing Miss Williams in class would be bad enough. Even if she was nice to me, which she probably would be because she'd feel sorry that anybody could be so pitiful, it'd still be bad. In fact, it might even be better if she just came out and told me how she couldn't believe I could be such an idiot.

Twice during the night I'd woke up in this wicked sweat with this awful sense of doom, and both times I got out of bed and did sit-ups and push-ups until my stomach and arms ached, hoping maybe I could snap back into that feeling I'd had on Friday. It didn't work. In the morning I didn't even hear my alarm go off, and when Mom finally woke me up, I felt like I'd been run over by a steamroller.

"Up and at 'em!" Mom said in her usual cheerful morning voice. "Time to face the new day!"

I groaned.

My head was still in a cloud when I got to school. Which isn't that unusual for me on a Monday morning, but this time I was out of it even by *my* standards. Luckily, the first kid I had to deal with turned out to be Mary Grace. Her locker's next to mine, and she was waiting for me when I got there. If there was anybody who wouldn't give me a hard time, it'd be Mary Grace.

"Hi, Tyler," she said and kind of just stood there looking at me.

"Hi, Mary Grace." As I plunked my bookbag down and started opening my locker, I could still feel her eyes on me. Even after I got the locker open, she didn't dig in and start helping me sort out what I'd need, which she generally did, especially on a Monday when I could barely even remember what classes I had, let alone what we were doing in them. She just stood there looking.

"What?" I said after I'd grabbed a few books and stuffed my bookbag into the locker. "What?"

"Nothing," she said, and I could see she was trying to work her face into a normal-looking smile. "I'm just waiting to walk to homeroom with you."

"But you were *looking* at me," I told her. "My mother does that, and it drives me crazy."

"Sorry," she said. "I didn't know I couldn't look at you." She kept looking at me.

"You heard what happened, didn't you?" I said. It came out more like an accusation than a question. I set my jaw. "Come on, say it. I can tell from the way you're acting. You know, don't you?"

She nodded. "Yeah, I heard."

I threw up my arms and paced back and forth for a few seconds. "How'd you find out?"

"Babette told me," she said.

"Babette!" I squeaked. "Oh, God, my life is ruined!" I leaned back against my locker and slid down till I was sitting on the floor. "How'd Babette find out?"

"From Sher."

I grabbed my head and squeezed. I couldn't believe it. The two people in the whole world who I least wanted to find out about this already knew. I closed my eyes and rapped the back of my head against my locker a few times. "How'd Sher find out?" I said between my teeth.

"He saw," Mary Grace said. "He saw it for himself."

I opened my eyes.

"He saw?" I said. "He saw?" I got this awful picture in my mind of Sher hiding in our shrubs on Thanksgiving Day and spying on our dinner. I couldn't believe it. Not even Sher could be that mad over one little fight, could he?

"He saw *them*," Mary Grace said. "Together."

"Oh, God," I said. "He *was* there." I didn't know if I should fight him again or quit school. Or both.

"He was where?" Mary Grace wanted to know. "Are we talking about the same thing?"

I looked up at her. "What are *you* talking about?"

"Miss Williams and Chuckie Deegan. What do you think? Sher saw them together Saturday night at Willie's."

Willie's was a restaurant on Main Street that was big in July and August with the Saratoga racing crowd. By November it was pretty quiet, the kind of candlelit place that Chuckie'd bring a date to.

"That's it?" I said. Part of me was still jealous of Chuckie, picturing them both at Willie's, but another part of me was almost doing cartwheels inside because that meant Sher and everybody didn't really know what happened on Thanksgiving.

"I was afraid you'd be upset," Mary Grace said. "You know..."

"It's a free country. They're adults." I stood up.

"*Consenting* adults, from what I heard." That wasn't Mary Grace. It was Jason, who had suddenly appeared out of nowhere. "Give it up, Ty. They were all over each other."

Then I heard kissing sounds, and Sher's head popped up right behind Jason's. "They were sucking face, bay-bee!" He gave a sneery little laugh, but I noticed he stayed behind Jason like he thought I might attack again. "As soon as they got into his car, they started sucking face, big time."

"And knowing you," I said, "you were probably sitting on the hood with your face plastered up against the windshield."

"You lose, Ty," Jason said. "Nice try, but no cigar."

"I never said I owned her," I told him. "What's the big deal?" I turned to go to homeroom.

"Hey, Ty."

I looked back. It was Jason. He looked all serious and had his finger pointed in the air. "Better to have loved and lost than never to have loved at all," he told me.

"Funny," I said as Jason and Sher cracked up. "Real funny."

Dealing with those guys at my locker turned out to be the best part of my day. I'd started out with two main worries: facing the kids and facing Miss Williams. I'd made it through the facing the kids part in one piece, so that left me the rest of the day to agonize over the facing Miss Williams part. And it wouldn't be so easy with her because she knew what *really* happened. I cringed whenever I thought about what kind of a jerk she must've thought I was. And I still ached when I thought about how beautiful she was and how she'd never feel the same way about me as I did about her.

At lunch I was trying to think what was the best way to go to science class—early to see Miss Williams and get it over with, or with the rest of the class so she wouldn't have to talk to me. Lymie thought I was depressed from finding out how

Chuckie'd been seen with Miss Williams, and he tried to cheer me up.

"Look at it this way, Ty," he said. "You're thirteen years old, and Chuckie's what...twenty-two, twenty-three? And he's in good shape and decent looking. You gotta expect that when somebody like that comes along, you're gonna get dumped." And all while he was telling me this he was stuffing a hamburger and French fries in his mouth. He hadn't hit his weight goal yet, but he figured he was working out enough so he could eat like an idiot again. "You should consider yourself lucky that she even looked at you in the first place."

"Thanks, Lyme," I told him.

"Listen," Lymie said. "I'm not done. What's the one advantage you got over Chuckie, huh? Think about it."

I thought. "Money? My family has more money."

Lymie lit up. "I hadn't even thought of that," he said. "But that's true. Having major bucks can't hurt. But what I meant was you got the advantage of time on your side."

I looked at him. "Time?"

"Look," he said, waving a hamburger at me, "when you're Chuckie's age, you'll still be in your prime, and Chuckie'll be over the hill. And if you put some muscle on and grow out of that goofy face, maybe *you'll* be stealing women from *him*." He grabbed some French fries off my tray, which he always did since they come with lunch and I never eat them anyway.

"Get real, Lyme," I told him. "Even if I believed in listening to you—which I don't—when I'm Chuckie's age, he'll only be like thirty-two. You call that over the hill?"

"Kind of," Lymie said. "Men reach their peak earlier than women. A guy's at his peak at around seventeen or eighteen, and a woman doesn't hit hers till she's over thirty. So when you're older, if you're still interested, you might be able to steal her back. You'll both be at your peaks."

Lymie got that kind of information off those afternoon talk shows he used to watch before heading out to do his evening chores. Now that wrestling season had started, I figured he'd go back to thinking about normal things. But I had to admit, some of the things he'd tell me about those shows would catch my attention, and this was one of them. If what he said was true, then in only four or five years I'd have another shot at Miss Williams. A real shot this time. Man to woman. So that made me feel a little better. But it was kind of depressing too. Peaking at eighteen? So when you graduated from high school, you'd get on this roller coaster which only went one way. Down. I sighed.

"So how do you think it started, Ty?" Lymie said. "When they were at your house, were they making goo-goo eyes across the table at each other or what?"

I rolled my eyes and didn't say anything.

"I mean, did you see it coming?" Lymie continued. "Or did it just hit you out of the blue?"

"See ya, Lymie," I said, getting up to go.

"Hey, not so quick," Lymie said, grabbing my arm.

I waited, wondering what else he had to say.

"Leave the fries," he said and slid them onto his plate.

Miss Williams was at her desk talking to a couple of kids when I got there. I'd decided to hang back at my locker so I could arrive at the last minute when things were usually a little hectic and I could slip into the classroom without being noticed. I'd caught Mary Grace starting to give me a funny look when she saw me at my locker because for weeks I'd practically flown to science class with no locker stop, but she didn't say anything, not even when I pretended to be looking for a pen, even though she was the kind of kid who carried enough pens to equip the whole class.

All while Miss Williams was taking attendance, I kept my head down and pretended to be finishing up some homework. A couple of times I felt like maybe she was looking at me, but I was afraid to check. I just sat there with my eyes frozen on my book.

Unfortunately for me it was lab day—the kind of day I used to look forward to because Miss Williams would go from lab station to lab station helping us with whatever we were doing. Especially the unscientific kids, which meant me. Because even though I'd spent the whole month practically memorizing every word that came out of Miss Williams's mouth, I still didn't know all that much about rocks, and she'd usually spend a lot of time at my station telling me about them. I didn't want that to happen now so I tried to concentrate while she was explaining the lab. Which wasn't that easy seeing how I was afraid to look up, and plus I was depressed. The lab was about metamorphic rocks, and we were supposed to match up different kinds of them with the rocks they were metamorphicized (or whatever you call it) out of, like the way marble was metamorphicized out of limestone. The last thing she said was that we'd be working in pairs and that we should each grab a partner.

I figured I could partner up with Mary Grace, who was a whiz at science, but before I even picked up my head to turn around and ask her, I felt something tugging at my arm. And unfortunately for me, it wasn't Mary Grace. It was Arliss Martin. Arliss was one of those Poindexter-looking kids who probably had an Einstein IQ, but around rocks forget it. He was as bad as I was.

Turning around, I noticed that Janey Adams had already hooked up with Mary Grace. What a waste. Both Janey and

Mary Grace were super-efficient types who could've done the whole lab by themselves. And you could have a busload of kids like me and Arliss and we'd still be lost.

"You think this is a good idea?" I asked Arliss.

"Hey," he told me. "Rocks are my life. I feel close to rocks. Some of my best friends are rocks."

I groaned. Arliss gave me this big grin and a thumbs up.

We grabbed the furthest lab station back, in the corner by the window. I wanted to be as far out of the way as possible, and Arliss wanted a lab station with a view. The first thing I noticed was that the rocks we were supposed to figure out, about twenty of them, were in one big pile. I was hoping they'd be in two rows and all we'd have to do was to match them. Which maybe I could handle if I was lucky. The next thing I noticed was all the stuff we were supposed to use to analyze them—the tools of the trade: a scratch plate, a file, a square of glass, a little bottle of acid, that kind of thing.

Arliss stuck a pair of goggles on his face. "So how do I look?" he wanted to know.

"They're you," I told him. "Now let's get going."

"Aye, aye, mon capitaine."

We both stood there and gawked at everything. Finally Arliss grabbed this shiny black rock out of the pile and held it up to his face.

"When you were zee little child, how did you feel about zee mother?" he said to the rock. "What's that you say? You wanted to kill zee father?"

"Cut it out," I said, "or we'll never get this done." He put the rock down.

"Scalpel," he said and laid his hand out in front of me.

I stuck a file in his hand and he scratched it on his rock a few times.

"This rock is very hard." He looked at me. "Stop me if I'm getting too technical." He scratched it on the glass. "Harder than glass." He held up the rock again. "And now for the final comparison..." He raked it across the side of my head.

"Cut it out!" I said, slapping his hand away and then rubbing my head. "We're never gonna get done."

"Need help getting started, guys?" That was Miss Williams. I kept my head down and stared at the pile of rocks.

"Now that's an understatement if I ever heard one," Arliss told her.

"What's the first thing you should do?" Miss Williams said softly.

"First?" Arliss said. "I guess first we'd like to see a wine list."

I still didn't look up, but I knew Miss Williams was giving him one of her sweet half smiles. "Maybe we could start by sorting them by color?" she said.

"Yes, yes," Arliss said.

I was already sorting rocks like crazy.

"And after that?..." Miss Williams paused to see if either of us had any ideas.

"Yes, yes?" Arliss said. "Don't stop. You were on a roll."

"And after that you might sort them by hardness or density—whatever you think would be the best way. And remember, you have your index of rocks in the back of your textbook. So let's see what you can come up with, hmm?"

"Hmmmm," Arliss said.

The rest of the period went pretty much like that. I sorted rocks and studied the index. Arliss helped a little and goofed around a lot, and Miss Williams came by every ten minutes or so to see how things were going. I'd hear her footsteps, and I could almost feel the shadow she made as she leaned over us. One time she even put her hand on my shoulder as she asked how we were doing. I kind of shrugged. I still couldn't look at her. I couldn't even make myself say anything.

"I'm sure that what my associate means," Arliss said, "is that we can use all the help we can get. Why don't I get you a chair?"

Luckily, she didn't go for the chair idea. She went to help some other kids.

At the end of class, Miss Williams announced for us to take our worksheets home and write up the lab for homework. When the bell rang and I was heading for the door, I could feel her eyes on me, and I was pretty sure she was going to call me back to discuss what happened on Thanksgiving. With every step I took I was surer, and I tried to decide whether I should pretend not to hear her or what—because there was no way I wanted to look her in the face and talk to her. I kept going.

I got so wrapped up in expecting to hear my name that I could hardly believe it when I found myself out in the hall. Home free. And I hadn't had to pretend that I didn't hear Miss Williams calling me because she hadn't said a word. I knew that I hadn't missed it because I'd been listening harder than I'd ever listened in my whole life. I'd've heard it even if she'd whispered my name. I stopped outside the door and thought for a minute. I can never figure myself out. I'd spent practically the whole day dreading the idea of having to face Miss Williams, and now I was standing around trying to figure out why she hadn't asked me to stay behind so she could talk to me. I should have felt relieved, but I didn't. I felt bad. Worse than bad. Terrible. Hurt. Miss Williams didn't even try to say anything to make me feel better. She didn't even care that much about how bad I felt.

I couldn't believe it.

Practice that afternoon was pretty much the same as usual except that Chuckie was gradually cranking up the intensity of the workout to make sure we'd be ready for our big meet on Wednesday. He was showing us all kinds of escapes and combinations for pinning kids, and his eyes never let up from prowling the place and making sure nobody was goofing around. Which nobody was as far as I could tell, except maybe Ox, and that was mainly to get Chuckie going, I think. And Chuckie yelled at me a few more times about overtraining, which was getting to be pretty routine. This time it was because every time I thought about Miss Williams not even bothering to talk to me, I'd almost start to cry. So I tried to put my whole mind on working out and wrestling. And it was paying off. I even did fairly decent against Roger Herrington. He'd looked over at Chuckie when I tried to partner up with him, and Chuckie had shrugged, so we both figured it was all right. Roger pinned me, but not as fast as he would have a few weeks earlier. I even almost got him with a takedown once.

At the end of the practice, Chuckie sat us down and gave us this big speech—one of those psych-up speeches like you see in the movies. He told us this was the best workout we'd had yet, and as far as he was concerned there wasn't a wrestling team in the whole area that was in as good a shape as we were. "You train like a madman, and only a madman can beat you," he told us again. "And believe me, there's nobody around here who trains like you guys. Look at this guy," he continued, walking over and pointing at me. "Our smallest guy—he's only in eighth grade—and he's working out so hard if I didn't stop him, he'd kill himself. And that's the attitude I see around here, and that's why Wednesday those guys aren't gonna know what hit 'em. It won't matter what they try on you. It's not gonna work."

"No effect, Coach!" Victor yelled, going up on his knees and flexing like the Incredible Hulk. "They ain't gonna have no effect."

“That’s right,” Chuckie said. “They won’t have a chance.”

“NO EFFECT! NO EFFECT!” Victor chanted and waved his arms for everybody to join in.

“They won’t be able to touch you guys!” Chuckie was strutting around now like he was General Patton or something.

“NO EFFECT! NO EFFECT!” Everybody was chanting now, even me and Lymie. It was the kind of thing that if you were to see a videotape of yourself doing it in one of your cooler moments, you’d feel like a jerk, but while you’re in the middle of it, it really seems like the thing to do. Chuckie’d shout something like, “They can’t hurt you!” and we’d all chant, “NO EFFECT!” Pretty soon Chuckie stopped saying stuff and just paced around while we chanted. We kept getting louder and louder, and I have to admit, it felt pretty good. Only we weren’t all chanting about the same thing. Everybody else was thinking mainly about the other wrestling team and how they wouldn’t be able to do anything to us. I was thinking about Miss Williams.

✧ XXI ✧

Most of Tuesday was like the flip side of Monday. All day long I was going out of my way to walk by Miss Williams's room, hoping I'd see her standing outside her door and that maybe she'd call me over and want to talk to me. I was pretty sure what she'd say. She'd tell me how much she appreciated me and liked having me around and all that, and how even though maybe she didn't like me the way I wanted her to, she hoped we could still be friends. I wasn't all that crazy about having to listen to that whole routine, but I figured the sooner we got it out of the way, the sooner things could gradually start to get back to normal. If things ever *did* get back to normal.

But I struck out. Every time I went past her room—which I did at least once between every period—she'd always be inside talking to some kids at her desk, or getting lab things out, or standing around looking out the window. I could've probably had a heart attack or something in the hall and she'd've been the last one to find out about it. So at lunch I took out my science book and tried to find something in it to ask her about.

What I'd have to do would be to get to class early enough so that she'd be able to answer my science question and still have enough time left over for her speech about liking me but not the way I wanted. Even with Lymie bugging me all through lunch, I still came up with what I thought was a pretty decent question—one that looked real but wouldn't take too long to answer. And I'd have to bring all my science stuff to sixth period so that as soon as the bell rang I could shoot out of there and get to Miss Williams's room before anybody else.

Which I did. So forty-five minutes later, I was outside Miss Williams's door rehearsing my question—which was about glaciers—and taking one last huge breath before I stepped into the room. An empty room. Miss Williams was nowhere to be seen.

I groaned and plunked my books down on my desk. Now what? Within two or three minutes, other kids would start arriving and Miss Williams wouldn't have any chance to talk to me privately. I sat down and kept watching for her to come through the door. If she showed up right away, and if I dropped my phony glacier question and just walked up to her desk and said hello, she'd probably have time for her spiel. Or if she didn't, she might at least ask me if I could stay after class so we could talk some more. That'd mean I'd be late for wrestling practice, but it'd be worth it. I tapped my foot and kept watching the door. Still no Miss Williams. Just my luck. This was the first time I could ever remember that she wasn't in her room when I got there. And I used to be there before anybody.

When the first kids came through the door, I gave it up completely. I figured it'd be yesterday all over again. I'd feel uncomfortable all during the class, and Miss Williams would keep looking at me, kind of wanting me to say something maybe, but not being able to with twenty other kids sitting around gawking at us.

Pretty soon the bell rang and Miss Williams still wasn't there. Mary Grace sat down behind me and poked me in the back. "Where's Miss Williams?" she said.

"How am I supposed to know?" As soon as I said it I realized I hadn't sounded very nice. Lymie and I talked like that to each other all the time, but with Mary Grace it was different. She was used to people being nice to her. "Sorry," I said, turning around. "I haven't seen her."

I hardly even got done apologizing when I heard Miss Williams's voice. And it was saying *my* name. I looked at her in the doorway and saw she was holding a white pass in the air.

"Tyler," she said, "could you report to the guidance office?"

My jaw dropped down. Was she so disgusted with me that she was going to have me moved out of her class? I couldn't believe it. I hardly even remember getting up there, but the next thing I knew I was taking the pass from her in the doorway.

"Check back later, Tyler, if you have time, and I'll tell you what you missed." She gave me a smile, but I was pretty sure it was strained. On my way by, she gave my shoulder a little squeeze.

All the way down to guidance, I kept worrying about what was up. In a way, I was glad it was guidance and not the main office that wanted me. I remembered how Buck Tracy got sent for by the main office one time because his house had just burnt down. And the guidance office only handled schedules and that kind of thing. I thought more about that and realized it wouldn't do any good for Miss Williams to kick me out of her earth science class because she was the only eighth-grade science teacher, and even if they took me out of earth science, they'd have to put me in one of her general science classes. Plus

Miss Williams had just told me to check back with her to get my work, and she wouldn't have done that if she was kicking me out.

I looked down at my pass. All of a sudden my feet stopped. My breathing too. I leaned up against the wall and looked at it again. The pass wasn't from my guidance counselor. It was from Bob Chirillo. The group therapy guy with the walkie-talkie. I was being sent down there for counseling. Miss Williams must've told them I was crazy.

Bob and I sat there for a minute looking at each other. I was almost crying. I still couldn't believe Miss Williams would send me there.

"Do you know why you're here?" Bob said finally.

I shrugged.

"Do you know who referred you?"

I shrugged again and just sat there. Bob sat there too, only he didn't have his head down like I did. I could feel him studying me.

"Miss Williams," I said finally and slumped down further in my chair.

"You got it," Bob said. "And why do you suppose she referred you here?" He rocked back in his chair and put his hands behind his head, studying me some more.

"Did she tell you?" I asked weakly.

"I'm more interested in what you have to tell me," he said.

It was quiet for a while. I was trying not to cry. Plus I didn't know what to say.

"You like Miss Williams?" Bob said after a few minutes. He leaned forward and twisted his face into something that was supposed to say "I care."

I couldn't really tell what he meant by "like," but it didn't really matter. I just wanted to get it over with and get out of there.

"Yeah," I said. "I like her."

"You like her more than as a teacher..." He didn't say it like a question. And his face was caring harder than ever.

"I don't know," I told him. "I like her."

Pause.

"And you invited her to dinner."

"Kind of."

Another pause. I was busy looking at my feet but I could feel his eyes on the top of my head.

"About the dinner. Why did you invite her?"

I shrugged. "I don't know. I wanted her to come."

"Because you like her. You like her so you wanted her to come to dinner."

I squirmed in my chair a little and then I shrugged again.

"You don't need to feel guilty about this," Bob told me. "We're not about judging here." He waited again. For quite a while.

"Yeah," I said. "I invited her because I like her."

"And how do you feel about that now?"

I thought for a minute. "You mean do I feel like it was wrong?"

He shook his head. "We're not about right and wrong here. We're about getting in touch with feelings and making appropriate decisions."

I sat there some more. I didn't know what he wanted from me, and I felt too lousy to even care that much.

Finally he talked again. "It's one of those gray areas, isn't it? Do you know what I mean when I say 'gray area'? That's when things aren't all black, and they aren't all white. They're gray. And those gray areas can get confusing. That's why it's beneficial to take time like this to sort out how we feel about these issues." He looked at me. "How would you describe your feelings right now? Happy? Sad? Confused? Depressed? Or what?"

I looked at my shoes again. "I don't know. Depressed maybe?"

"Good," he said. "That's good. Don't be afraid of your feelings. Get them out in the open. Share them." His "I care" face was getting happier now. He leaned forward and put his elbows on his desk. "How often would you say you feel that way?"

"Depressed?"

He nodded. He seemed pretty excited that we were actually going to talk about a feeling, even if it was a bad one.

"Every once in a while," I said. "Whenever it feels like everything is going wrong."

"So you've been depressed before," he said, leaning in closer to me. "Let me ask you a blunt question. Have you ever considered suicide?"

"Suicide?"

"Suicide," he said, staring me right in the eye. "Tell me the truth. Have you ever considered it?"

I shook my head. "No," I said. "Not really."

"Not really?" he said, leaning back in his chair and kind of squinting at me. "How can you 'not really' think about something?"

I shrugged. He leaned forward on his desk again. He even peeked over at the closed door like he was making sure nobody was spying on us or anything.

"The fact is you *have* thought of suicide," he said, staring at me so hard it was like he was trying to see right into my brain. "Let's be totally honest with each other. There's only the two of us. We don't judge here. There's no need to hide behind some kind of mask that says 'All my thoughts are positive. I never feel terrible. I never feel self-destructive.'"

He was quiet for a while. I was too. Then he started in again. "Let's play a little game here. Let's take that judge that sits inside your head and set him off to the side for a while." He took his hands and acted like he was setting the judge off to the side. "All right?"

"Yeah," I said. What was I supposed to do—ask him to put it back when we both knew there wasn't anything there anyway?

"Tell me honestly—the judge is over here now, and he can't hear you—have you ever thought that you wanted to die, that maybe you'd be better off dead?"

I thought about how miserable I felt when my father died and how peaceful he looked at the wake. And I remember thinking how it might be easier just to be dead like that and not have to worry about anything anymore.

"Yeah," I said, "I've thought that."

"Good," Bob said. "Very good." He leaned in closer to me. "And how would you do it?"

I looked at him. "Huh?" I thought I knew what he meant but I figured I must be wrong.

"Kill yourself," he said. "How would you go about it?"

I was right. But I still kind of flinched when he said it.

"I wouldn't," I told him.

"But you just told me you've thought about it. What's it gonna be? You either have or you haven't. You can't have it both ways."

"Then I haven't," I said, squirming a little.

Bob gave this big sigh. "What I'm trying to do here is to cut through all the phony-baloney most of us hide behind and get right down to the nitty-gritty. I can tell by your body language that I've struck a nerve, so let's stay honest and follow through on this and see where we end up." He squinted at me again. "When you get those feelings that you'd be better off dead, how do you see that happening? How do you see yourself going from Point A to Point B?"

"I don't," I told him, wondering how I'd ever convince him that I really didn't want to go to Point B, at least not for another sixty or seventy years.

"Come on. Help me through that wall you're hiding behind. Would you use a gun? Cut your wrists?"

I'd never even touched a real gun, and I didn't really want to. And just the thought of somebody cutting their wrists made me want to throw up. This was not my kind of conversation.

"Look," I said, staring right at him and trying not to raise my voice, "I don't go around thinking about killing myself. I swear to God I don't. And anyway, I wouldn't use guns or razors or anything on myself. I don't even like getting shots."

"Pills?" he said. "Go to sleep and never wake up?"

"No!" I almost shouted at him. "I'm not killing myself!"

I was all ready for him to suggest that I turn on gas or breathe carbon monoxide or something, but he didn't. He started in again about openness and honesty and how my family was probably dysfunctional because most families really are, if everybody'd just admit it. And if I'd try to convince him that my mother was a good mother by telling him, say, how she grounded me for fighting, he'd say something like, "So there *is* some tension between you and your mother. You want to talk about that?"

What I wanted to do was get out of there. I was depressed *enough* when I arrived. When I left, I was practically a basket case. I finally even cried. Bob was all happy. He told me we made some good progress.

"Tomorrow," he said, "we'll really get busy."

✧

I was a half hour late for practice. "What's the matter with you?" Chuckie said as soon as I walked in.

"It's not my fault," I told him without even looking his way. "I had to go to the guidance office."

"I didn't ask where you were. I asked what was the matter with you."

"Nothing," I said.

He came over to where I was and looked me in the eye. "I know you," he said. "And when you get that pouty look on your face, it always means something's wrong. So why don't you just tell me what it is and save us both some time."

"Not you too!" I couldn't believe it. It was like being in one of those bad dreams where you're being chased by a bear or some deranged psychopath or something, and just when you think you've gotten away and you're safe, there he is standing by your side. Then something dawned on me. Something terrible. Probably Bob had already gotten to Chuckie and taught him how to counsel me. "I can't take any more of this," I said. "I'm going home."

I started off the stage, but within two seconds I felt this iron band clamp down on my arm. It was Chuckie's hand, and it pulled me back to where he was.

"Are you going to tell me what's wrong, or am I supposed to guess?"

"Go ahead," I told him. "Do what you're supposed to do. Ask me if I spend all my time thinking about guns and knives and jumping out windows."

Chuckie looked at me like I had two heads. "Did I miss something here?"

"Didn't Bob Chirillo tell you what to say to me?"

Chuckie studied me for a few seconds and then dragged me

over to this chair by the edge of the wrestling mat. He cranked on my arm until I was sitting on it.

"Switch partners," he yelled to everybody else. Then to me. "Who's Bob Chirillo?"

I looked up at him. "You really don't know?" I said. "No lie?"

"I really don't know," he said. "And that's why you're gonna tell me." He squatted down alongside my chair. "Well?"

I really didn't want to go into the whole thing, but I was pretty sure Chuckie wasn't going to let me drop it. Besides, it might feel good to talk to somebody normal after being locked up for more than a hour with Bob Chirillo. So I started in. I told him about Miss Williams sending me down to Bob, and about everything Bob and I had talked about, and how I thought I'd never get out of there. The team had to switch partners three times before I got done.

"So that's what's wrong with me," I said finally. "First I get stood up at dinner—kind of. Then Miss Williams decides I'm crazy and sends me to counseling. And then I spend the rest of the afternoon talking to this guy who isn't gonna be happy unless I tell him I want to kill myself so he can counsel me out of it."

Chuckie started to chuckle.

"What's so funny?" I said, glaring at him.

"I'm not laughing at you," he said. "It's just the situation. You know how every once in a while you read about a fireman who runs around torching buildings so he can put the fires out."

"Yeah, well it's not so funny if you're the one getting torched," I told him.

"Don't take it personally," he said. "You're probably just another notch on that guy's desk. Another life saved from a bad mood." He paused. "But you're wrong about Aileen—Miss Williams. She doesn't think you're crazy. She likes you a lot.

She knew you felt bad over what happened, and she probably wasn't sure about the best way to handle it."

"So she sends me to that guy? Yeah, she must really like me a lot. My permanent record card probably says not to seat me next to windows now."

Chuckie smiled. "I'll talk to her tonight."

"Tell her I'm not going back to that guy. 'Cause I'm not."

"Don't worry about it. I doubt that she'll want you to when she hears how it went." He stood up. "Now tell me the truth. If I send you to the locker room to get dressed for practice, will you promise me you won't try to slam a locker door shut on your head or scald yourself in the shower room?" He cocked an eyebrow and looked down at me.

I thought about belting him in the arm but he looked so funny I didn't.

"Maybe I'll just stay here and keep staring at you till *that* kills me," I told him.

"Witty," he said. "Very witty." And he picked me up by the head until I was standing up. "Hurry back. Ox has been wanting to partner up with you, and today I might just let him do it."

By the time I got back to the mat, nobody was getting too much of a workout. Chuckie wanted to keep us busy so we'd stay sharp, but he also wanted to make sure we'd be rested up for our meet the next day. He spent the whole rest of the practice reviewing takedowns and escapes and combinations for pins, that kind of thing, and then right before we left he sat us down and started telling different ones of us about the kids we'd be wrestling and giving hints about where they might be weak and what kinds of situations to avoid and where to come on strong. Most of the varsity guys already seemed to know who they'd be wrestling from last season, but they still listened pretty close and nodded whenever Chuckie told them something. I waited for him to give me some tips about my guy, but he never did.

"What about Ty's guy?" Lymie finally said. Lymie still hadn't quite made 105, which is where he could have had a shot at varsity, so he'd be sitting out the first meet.

"Yeah, Coach," Ox said with this big happy face. "Ain't you gonna warn John Henry about The Slug?"

"Shut up, Ox!" That wasn't Chuckie. It was Victor, and he was wearing his usual Victor scowl. "He's been working hard, so leave 'im alone." He looked at me. "You'll do all right. Don't worry."

All of a sudden I was seriously worried. When somebody like Victor starts sticking up for you, it makes you stop and think.

"I didn't say he wouldn't do all right," Ox said, his big face twisting into a little kid's pout.

"*Everybody'll* do all right," Chuckie said, "so don't anybody worry."

He kept talking for a while longer about other wrestlers and what to watch out for and all that, but he still didn't say anything about my guy. The Slug. I was really starting to wonder. Next thing I knew, we were all chanting "NO EFFECT! NO EFFECT!" again. I didn't even know who started it this time. I chanted along with everybody else, but I think it was harder for me to get into it. The kids who wouldn't be wrestling were pretty safe from any effect anyway, and the other varsity kids could kind of picture who it was that wasn't going to have any effect on them. Me, I could only imagine.

✧ XXII ✧

THE NEXT DAY we had weigh-ins before school. That was the only part of the whole deal I wasn't worried about. Most of the other guys had gone all night without eating or drinking anything, and they came early to try to sweat out some more weight. The way it worked was if they could make weight in the morning, then they'd be able to do whatever they wanted for the rest of the day as long as they didn't gain any more than three pounds before they had to weigh in at the meet itself.

I was the first one in the weigh-in line because I was in the lightest weight class. Mr. Johnson, the athletic director, was in charge of weighing us. He gave this chuckle when he saw me at the scale.

"Now there's confidence," he said, nodding his head at me.

I did look different from everybody else on the team. They were all standing around in their underwear, and a few of them weren't even wearing that, while I was standing there in a pair of jeans, a Bugle Boy sweatshirt, and my Adidas. I even still had my ski hat on.

Mr. Johnson set the weights for 91, and I stepped on. The bar floated up to the top. I couldn't believe it. I must've put on some weight. Muscle, I hoped.

"We'll fix that," I heard Chuckie say, and then he grabbed my hat off and yanked my sweatshirt up over my head. The bar floated back down.

The other guys all stepped onto the scale like they were walking on eggshells, but they all made it—except Justin, who was going for 98. He had to get back into his sweat suit and do laps around the gym, then come back in and get completely dried off before he made it. Just barely. The bar was floating right up near the top.

When I stepped outside the locker room, the last person I expected to almost bump into was Miss Williams. But there she was.

"You waiting for Chuckie?" I said, kind of surprised.

"I was waiting for you," she told me. "Can we talk?"

I shrugged. "I guess."

"My room?" she said, putting her hand on my shoulder.

I looked up at the clock. There were ten minutes left before the kids would start arriving for homeroom.

"I heard how it went yesterday," Miss Williams said. "Chuckie told me."

We were sitting face to face, both of us in students' desks in the front of the room. I hadn't really said anything the whole way there, other than nodding my head and giving an occasional "yeah." Now that we were face to face I still didn't say anything. I wasn't trying to be mean. I just couldn't think of anything.

"I'm sorry it went badly," she said. "I was hoping it would help."

I tried to smile. "It wasn't that bad."

"Can you ever forgive me?"

I nodded. "You didn't know what that guy was like." I looked down at my desk. "It's just..."

"It's just what?" Miss Williams wanted to know.

I shrugged. "I don't know. It's just that...why didn't you want to talk to me yourself? Why'd you have to send me to somebody else?"

It was quiet for a few seconds. I was staring down at my desk, so I couldn't tell if I'd made her mad or what. But I was glad I'd told her the truth. Finally, I heard her sigh.

"I've been wracking my brain trying to figure out the same thing since I talked to Chuckie last night. I keep wondering why I didn't keep you after class to talk to you, which was my first impulse. I tried to explain it to Chuckie—and myself too—I think, and I'm pretty sure neither of us was very well convinced. If you don't mind, I'll try to explain it to you."

"No," I said, meaning I didn't mind.

"I'm still new in this business," she told me. "Other than student teaching, I've only been in the classroom for a few weeks. But I've known I wanted to be a teacher since I was your age, and for the past five years I've been preparing for it." She paused. "You know, Tyler, you probably think that when we teachers were in college, we mostly studied the subjects we planned on teaching. But a lot of what we studied had to do with learning how to teach more effectively and how to communicate better and how to handle different classroom situations. In fact, I probably spent more time studying that kind of thing than I did studying science."

"You're a good teacher," I said when she paused again, "so it must've worked."

"Thanks," she said. "That means a lot to me coming from

you. It really does." She gave me a little smile. "Anyway, we learned technique after technique to make us better teachers and more effective communicators and so on, all of which *seems* like a good idea, and in a lot of ways it probably is..." She paused and looked me right in the eye. "But I'm starting to wonder if we aren't sacrificing something—something natural and human—by looking at teaching and communication as sciences made up of techniques and strategies. Maybe all this in some way clutters our thinking and makes it easy for us to forget how to just talk to each other, how to simply deal with each other as people. I'm probably rambling a little, but does this make any sense to you so far?"

I nodded. "My mother read this book one time, and it told you how to talk to your kids the right way, so afterwards, instead of saying things like 'Why do you have to be such a slob?' or 'You oughta be ashamed to leave your room in that condition,' she'd have to say something like 'When you leave wet towels and dirty clothes on the floor, I feel frustrated and angry.'"

Miss Williams smiled. "And how did that work?"

"She's back to asking me why I've gotta be such a slob," I said, and we both laughed.

"I'm reassured that someone as accomplished as your mother is struggling with the same kinds of problems I am," Miss Williams said, and then she thought for a few seconds before continuing with her explanation. "Another thing we learned in college was that since we could never possibly hope to become an expert in all areas of dealing with students, when we see situations that we're not trained to handle, we should rely on our support services. For instance, if we see a student who appears to be straining to hear what we're saying or to see the board, we should send him to someone who can diagnose the problem and help him. And if we see a student who's upset about something or appears to be unhappy..."

"Like me after Thanksgiving."

"Like you after Thanksgiving." She stopped and seemed to grope for words. "I wanted to talk to you, but I was afraid that I might say the wrong thing—afraid I might make things worse. Can you understand that?"

I nodded. "I didn't know what to say to you either."

Miss Williams looked me in the eye. "Sooo...knowing there was somebody on the staff trained to deal with students' personal problems..."

"You figured I should go to him."

"Exactly." She seemed to study me to see how I was taking all this.

"I was afraid you thought I was crazy or something."

She smiled and reached over and put her hand on my hand. I felt this tingle go all through me.

"How could I ever think you were crazy? Tyler, if I teach in this school for the next hundred years, I don't expect to ever have a student whom I think more highly of than I do you. You are absolutely wonderful."

"They'd probably make you retire before then," I said smiling.

She smiled too and gave my hand a little squeeze. "And about dinner at your house...When I found out that *you* had actually invited me, instead of simply trying to make me feel welcome as Chuckie's guest, I felt terrible, but that's only part of what I felt. I also felt honored. I really did. And I still feel that way."

"So does that mean you're gonna drop Chuckie?" I cocked an eyebrow so she'd know I was only kidding.

That cracked her up. "Well," she said, "we don't want to

hurt Chuckie's feelings, now do we?"

I shook my head. "Then we'd have to send *him* down to see Bob Chirillo."

"*That* I'd like to see. Wouldn't you love to be a fly on the wall during that session?"

I smiled just thinking about it. I wondered what Chuckie would say to a guy like Bob. Or if he'd end up belting him.

"Miss Williams?" I said after a while. "What's that guy's problem? Why's he always acting like everybody needs to be counseled about everything? And why's he gotta make people talk about suicide? Do you think *he's* crazy?"

"I don't think so. And I think he really *was* trying to help. Suicide among young people *has* been a growing problem. Last year when I was student teaching, we had an in-service workshop about suicide, and one of the things we were told was that if we find somebody who's thinking about doing it, we should confront them and ask really blunt questions about how they'd go about it. I suppose the idea is to force them to confront the reality of it and then help them work out less drastic alternatives."

"And Bob Chirillo was at that workshop?"

There was a slight pause and a sheepish smile. "He was running it."

"Figures."

"In fairness to Mr. Chirillo, I have seen pamphlets on the subject which advise pretty much the same thing." She smiled. "But in this case, I think he may have gotten a little carried away, hmm?"

"Just a speck, maybe. He was almost passing out weapons."

She laughed. "My father still reminds me that common sense always runs the risk of being overruled by a little education. Which, I must say, was what I was guilty of. I should have talked to you myself."

"You think he'll put it on my permanent record card that I want to kill myself?"

She shook her head. "I don't think so. But if it makes you feel better, I'll check on it personally."

"It would. Nothing that guy does to drum up business would surprise me."

"Don't worry. I'll talk to him."

"And could you…could you make sure I don't have to see him again? I think he's got me penciled in for the rest of the decade."

"Done," she said. "That's the least I can do."

"Thanks," I said. "I mean it." And I didn't just mean for checking my permanent record card and canceling my appointments. I meant for everything.

She squeezed my hand again. "And thank you for listening to me. I really enjoy talking to you."

I almost floated up out of my chair.

✧ XXIII ✧

OUR MEET WAS at six o'clock. Which left more than three hours after school for me to work up a pretty good case of nerves. The school day itself had been pretty decent—more than decent even. After talking to Miss Williams, it was like this weight had been lifted off me. For one thing, I didn't feel like some mental case anymore, or even that pathetic. And for another thing, I didn't have to worry about Bob Chirillo and his walkie-talkie coming after me and marching me to his office for more counseling. And for a third thing Miss Williams still seemed to like me.

When I got home and went up to my room, the first thing I saw was my uniform hanging from a hanger on my doorknob. Chuckie had given them out to all the varsity kids after practice the day before. When I'd first held it up, I thought Chuckie'd made a mistake because it was so small. Only he hadn't made any mistake because it turned out to be pretty stretchable. The label didn't say what it was made out of, but Mom told me it seemed to be some kind of nylon polyester blend. She said it with this "I knew nothing good would come out of this wrestling business" look on her face. Mom was big into natural fibers.

"We can only guess how many chemicals went into this thing," she said, holding it at arm's length like it might grab her or something.

"I'm gonna wear it, Mom, not eat it," I told her.

She studied it for another minute before deciding it should be washed, even though it already seemed pretty clean to me, so that was the last I saw of it until now. It didn't look any cleaner than before, but it did look like it'd been ironed. Which seemed like a pretty useless thing to do since my match would be the first one and before hardly anybody got to see it, it'd be rolling around the mat with somebody called The Slug. Just thinking about this Slug kid sent a shiver up my spine. I even thought about calling Chuckie and asking him why he hadn't told me stuff about The Slug. But I didn't for the same reason I didn't ask him on the way home from practice the day before. I was afraid he'd think I was afraid. Which I was, kind of.

Mom made me come down and get something to eat at three-thirty since she knew I couldn't eat any dinner before my match. It was only some tomato soup (fresh, because fresh food is another thing Mom is into) and some saltines (nonfat), but I still had a hard time getting it down because I had stomach butterflies something fierce. I could feel Mom kind of studying me all while I sat at the kitchen table.

"Are you sure you're all right?" she said finally. "I don't like the way you look."

"I can't help how I look," I told her, even though I knew what she meant.

"I mean you look pale. You might be coming down with something." She came over and started feeling my head. "You don't feel hot," she said.

"'Cause I'm not sick." I was surprised that part of me was almost hoping that I did have some disease.

"Don't worry, Linda," Mrs. Saunders said. "Chuckie will look out for him." Then she started studying me with that same worried look Mom had.

Neither of them were helping me any. I kept thinking about two things: number one—that I'd be killed, and number two—that I'd be humiliated, which I think scared me more than being killed. I mean, what if this Slug kid took one look at me, shook his head with disgust, and then just rammed my shoulders into the mat for the pin? And I'd have to walk back to my team's side in this neatly pressed wrestling uniform to the sound of everybody groaning. I even found myself hoping that if he was going to do that, he'd at least give me a decent enough injury so people there would be able to work up some sympathy for me. You know things are pretty bad when you're actually hoping you'll get seriously hurt. Maybe Bob was right about me.

When I got back to my room, I all of a sudden remembered about Miss Williams being at the meet, and I almost threw up what little tomato soup and crackers was in me. Why did I ever invite her? What was I, crazy or something? (I thought of Bob again.) Miss Williams was the last one who I wanted to see me get totally humiliated. I paced back and forth across my room about seven hundred times. Then I sat down, figuring I should save my strength, but after about a minute I found myself back up on my feet wearing out more carpet.

Next I decided to try on my uniform again. I'd already tried it on quick before Mom snagged it, just to make sure it fit, but now I wanted to see exactly how I'd look out there. I slid out of my clothes and stepped into the thing and pulled up the shoulder straps. Next I slid my knee pads on, and then my Asics

Tiger wrestling shoes—all stuff which Chuckie had helped me pick out. Finally, I snapped on the headgear and trudged over to the mirror and started studying myself.

First off, I couldn't believe how young I looked. Which wasn't all that terrible in this case—it might soften the crowd. But besides looking like some ten-year-old, I had to admit I didn't look all that bad. I studied my arms. I was actually getting some definition there. No ripples or popping veins like my brother Chris or Chuckie, but at least you could tell I was getting into halfway decent shape. I scowled into the mirror, trying to look lean and mean. It didn't work. I looked more like some little kid about to throw a wicked tantrum.

By the time we got back to the school for the final weigh-in, I was more nervous than ever. Chuckie'd hardly talked at all in the car, and the last thing he said before we got out was, "You'll do all right." But he still didn't say anything about The Slug. And I still didn't ask.

The only good thing was Mom wasn't coming to the meet. As the afternoon wore on, I realized she was almost more nervous about the whole thing than I was, and when I told her she didn't have to come, she argued a little, but I think she was relieved. So at least I wouldn't have to worry about her doing something seriously embarrassing like running out on the mat and yelling at The Slug for being rough or something. But now as we were all milling around waiting for the other team to show up, I felt kind of like an orphan. Chuckie was busy checking to see if certain kids had made weight again, and everybody else seemed to have stuff to do like taping up their knees or setting up the scoring table or showing the scorekeepers what they were supposed to be doing—things like that. I just sat there and worried some more.

Lymie showed up at quarter to six. He wasn't wrestling. He was just there to cheer the rest of us on. The other team hadn't arrived yet. I was kind of hoping their bus had broken down. Three minutes later Lymie poked me and said, "Ty, there they are." He said it like we were cowboys or something and about a million Indians had just come over the ridge.

We stood in two lines in front of the scale—The Slug at the head of his line, and me at the head of ours. Ever since the other team had arrived, I'd been sneaking peeks at him. I couldn't believe my eyes. He was one of the most amazing things I'd ever seen. My imagination couldn't even have come up with something like him. He was almost a head shorter than me, but standing around in his underwear like he was, you could tell he was built like a brick wall. He had this round face that reminded me of Yoda from those *Star Wars* movies—if Yoda had an arrest record, that is—and he had these patchy-looking bald spots all over his head. I couldn't tell if it looked more like some of his hair had been worn off from wrestling or if he had some kind of mange. Every time I'd sneak a peek at him, he'd be staring at me like we were two dogs and I'd just stolen his bone. That was probably to psych me out. Which it did. If I'd had any bone of his, I'd've given it back for sure.

Chuckie and the other coach were behind the scale, watching the referee set the balance for 94 before motioning for us to step up to be weighed. The Slug edged me out and got up on the scale. I didn't know if this was because the visiting team always got to go first or whether he was just trying to show me who was boss. I watched as the bar started to rise, hoping like anything it'd keep going right up to the top, but before it got there, The Slug reached into his mouth and pulled out a dental plate with his two front teeth attached and set it on the frame of the scale. I don't even think he did it so he'd weigh less. I think he just wanted to be able to give me this gummy smile that wasn't a smile at all when the bar came to a stop.

I looked at Chuckie and kind of groaned. Only inside so nobody heard anything.

I don't remember watching all the other kids get weighed. The next thing I remember was charging out with the rest of the team and following Victor through our warm-up routine, and after that seeing The Slug doing one armed push-ups during his team's warm-ups. I looked over and saw Scott Malecki sitting in the first row of the bleachers. He waved and gave me the thumbs up with his good arm. I tried not to think about his broken one. Then I saw Miss Williams. She gave me a little smile before she went and sat down in the bleachers about five rows back, off to the side from where we were sitting. About thirty other people, mostly parents but some kids, were already sitting there. When Miss Williams got seated, she gave me another smile. I tried to smile back. I almost managed it too, until I looked back at The Slug. He was spinning around on his head just like Chuckie had done for us when he first took over our practices. I gave another silent groan. Chuckie's hand came down on my shoulder. I know it's not what he meant, but his hand seemed to be saying to me, "It's been nice knowing you."

"Go get 'im, Ty!" I heard all these voices saying behind me. My whole team was on their feet, all excited. Which was understandable since this was our first match of the first meet of the season. I hoped I wouldn't let them down. Or get killed. Or humiliated. The Slug and I met in the center and shook hands. And he showed me some more gums.

"Show him what you're made of, Ace." That was Chuckie.

Only I didn't really know what I was made of right then, even though my legs felt kind of like rubber as I circled around waiting to tie up with The Slug.

"Pin 'im, Ty!" That was Lymie, and it seemed like a funny thing to say, seeing how except for the handshake we hadn't even touched each other yet. But I didn't have much time to think about it. The Slug charged in and grabbed me by the back of the neck and the elbow, and I grabbed him back the same way. I don't even think I was scared anymore. All my attention was being used up keeping my weight centered so The Slug couldn't take me down. He drove in for a leg and missed. I skipped back with him without leaning out of balance. The Slug's patchy head stayed down, and kind of a growling sound started coming from the bottom side of it. But I didn't care. My mind stayed with my balance.

Next he yanked me forward. I went with him, still not in any danger. Then he jerked me to the side, and like a shot he was after my leg again. I skipped back with him, and he missed again. I started to think how if I could just keep my attention on my balance, he wouldn't be able to take me down—ever. He yanked on me some more, and I went with him like a rag doll—a perfectly centered rag doll. The Slug's breathing had become one long growl. I figured maybe he was losing his cool since he couldn't trick me off balance.

Next thing I knew, the ref was giving me a warning for stalling. I'd been concentrating so hard on keeping out of trouble, I'd almost forgotten I was supposed to be wrestling. We tied up again and I tried to put some attention on The Slug's balance, hoping to find an opening for an attack. Which I couldn't find. Even when he ducked in for a leg or something, he felt as solid and steady as a steamroller. The ref said something about stalling again. I had to do something.

The Slug lunged into me one more time, and I went with him the same as I'd been doing. But this time when he went to pull out, I came at him with all I had. It was like every muscle in my body was yelling "Geronimo!" Only The Slug wasn't there—not in front of me anyway—and the next thing I knew, I was riding an earthquake—the big one, the one I'd dreamed about as a kid and thought I'd missed when I moved out of California. The world was spinning out from under me. A crack of thunder shot through my head, and then I felt some air being knocked out of my lungs. After that, everything got quiet.

The next thing I knew, I saw Justin's out-of-focus face above me. He was looking at me like I was a ghost or something. Then Lymie's face was there. He looked at me the same way. I heard Chuckie's voice yell, "Don't move him!" and then his face appeared in front of Justin's and Lymie's.

I sucked in some air. "My back," I heard myself moan. I felt like I'd done a back flop on some jagged rock ledge.

"Let's see you move your feet," Chuckie said. He looked pretty worried.

I moved them.

"And your hands?"

I moved them too as other heads gathered around Chuckie's and Justin's and Lymie's. I twisted around so I could see why the floor under me hurt so much. "There's a chair under me," I said, puzzled, and started to sit up. I watched as Justin picked up the flattened-out folding chair that I'd landed on and started to open it up again.

Chuckie smiled. "If you broke it, you're paying for it." He grabbed my arm to steady me as I stood up, then pushed me back so I was sitting on the chair that Justin had just picked up. It was my own chair, at the end of the whole row of chairs for our team.

Chuckie pushed my head back and put a towel up to my nose. The towel instantly turned red. "Hold that up there, Ace. I don't think you hit your nose. It's just part of the overall jolt you took."

I stuck my hand up to the towel. My head hurt something fierce, and I groaned as I leaned back into my chair. The whole back of my body felt like one big bruise. I leaned forward a little and saw Victor and a few of the other guys glaring out onto the mat. Victor was clenching his fists. I looked where they were looking and saw The Slug. He was looking back at them. "He jucht flew," he said through his missing front teeth. He actually looked like he felt terrible.

"He does that," Roger Herrington told him, coming out in front of Victor and everybody. "Remember how *I* accidentally slammed ya, Ty?"

I nodded from behind my towel. I wasn't sure if that was such a great claim to fame. If I didn't watch it, I might end up being called That Flying Kid by the whole league.

"Let's get him into the locker room so I can take a look at him, Chuck. Just to be on the safe side." It was the doctor who'd given me the wrestling physical. I couldn't believe it. A doctor was there!

I felt some hands helping me up out of the chair, but before we headed for the locker room, Chuckie led me out onto the mat. The referee grabbed my hand and The Slug's hand and then lifted my hand high. I won. I figured there must be a rule about how far you can throw a kid off the mat.

"Sorry," The Slug said and patted me on the back. "Really."

As we turned toward the locker room, I was aware of something else. Cheering. Everybody in the bleachers was cheering like crazy. And some of them were girls. And they had worried looks on their faces. I looked further up in the bleachers. There was Miss Williams. She was cheering along with everybody else. When she saw me looking at her, she stood up and applauded some more. She tried to smile, but even from where I was I could see she had tears in her eyes. I couldn't believe it. The whole thing was like a dream.

"So what's it like winning your first match?" Chuckie said into my ear. "I didn't want you to know ahead of time, but that was last year's sectional champ you just wrestled."

I looked at him. "Yeah?" I said. I was glad I hadn't known.

"So how are you feeling?" Chuckie said as we entered the locker room. "You took quite a fall out there."

Almost before I finished the step I was taking, my whole last few weeks flashed across my mind. First I remembered Miss Williams and the Thanksgiving dinner and how terrible I'd felt about that. Then I remembered how nervous I'd felt about joining the wrestling team and how worried I was about my first match. And suddenly it dawned on me that I could hardly remember a time when I wasn't driving myself half crazy over one thing or another. It seemed like my whole life I'd been tossed from one problem to the next, one worry to the next—always struggling to land on my feet, but knowing there'd be times I'd end up crashing into a chair instead. It scared me a little thinking that, and thinking too, how things might always be like that. But in some strange way it felt good too—maybe just knowing I'd already made it this far and I was still in one piece. Kind of.

As I turned back to Chuckie I could still hear the last cheers from the crowd.

"No effect," I told him. I think I even managed a little smile.

DANIEL HAYES

lives in Schaghticoke, New York and teaches English at Troy High School. His previous books include *The Trouble with Lemons*, which was named an ALA Best Book for Young Adults and an IRA Young Adult Choice, and *Eye of the Beholder*.

NO EFFECT

has been set in Janson, an oldstyle face first issued by Anton Janson in Leipzig between 1660 and 1687, and typical of the Low Country designs broadly disseminated throughout Europe and the British Isles during the seventeenth century. The contemporary versions of this eminently readable and widely employed typeface are based upon type cast from the original matrices, now in the possession of the Stempel Type Foundry in Frankfurt, Germany.

Printed and bound by the Maple-Vail Book Manufacturing Group, Binghamton, New York.